The Last Notebook of Leonardo

Also by the author

Squiggle
Billy and the Birdfrogs

The Last Notebook of Leonardo

B. B. Wurge

A LeapKids Book
Leapfrog Kids
Leapfrog Press
Teaticket, Massachusetts

A LeapKids Book
Leapfrog Kids

Published in 2010 in the United States by
Leapfrog Press LLC
PO Box 2110
Teaticket, MA 02536
www.leapfrogpress.com

Printed in the United States of America

Distributed in the United States by
Consortium Book Sales and Distribution
St. Paul, Minnesota 55114
www.cbsd.com

First Edition

Library of Congress Cataloging-in-Publication Data

Wurge, B. B.
The last notebook of Leonardo / B.B. Wurge. -- 1st ed.
p. cm.
"A LeapKids Book."
Summary: Ten-year-old Jeremy's father, a genius inventor, turns himself into a giant orangutan and takes his son on an epic journey to discover the secrets of Leonardo Da Vinci.
ISBN 978-1-935248-14-9
[1. Inventors--Fiction. 2. Fathers and sons--Fiction. 3. Orangutans--Fiction. 4. Voyages and travels--Fiction. 5. Leonardo, da Vinci, 1452-1519--Fiction.] I. Title.
PZ7.W9656Las 2010
[Fic]--dc22

2010028865

For Ben

Dad with six fingers.

1

To tell you my story, I have to begin with my father. His name was Carl. For a long time, he worked for the government in a secret building underground. I think his office was in the sub-basement of a skyscraper in Manhattan. But he never told me exactly. He also never told me what he worked on. I am pretty sure he worked in a science lab discovering important and amazing things, secret things that the government wanted to keep for its own use.

One day he came home with a giant acid hole in his shoe. The entire front half of his shoe was gone. He seemed happy about it. Whatever had melted his shoe must have been an exciting discovery.

When I saw the damage, I was worried about his foot, but he said that he always wore Kevlar underwear, especially socks, because you never know when you might drop something nasty on your foot.

"Dad," I said. I was only seven at the time. "Should I wear Kevlar socks too? What if I spill grapefruit juice on my foot?"

"Don't worry about that, Jem," he said. Jem was short for Jeremy. "The compound I spilled today is a lot more interesting than grapefruit juice. In fact it burned right through the bottom of the flask, which is how I spilled it."

"What was it?" I said. "What were you trying to make?"

"Oh, never mind that," he said. "Tell me about your day at school." He always changed the subject whenever I got too nosey about his work.

A year later he came home with an extra finger on his hand. I didn't even notice at first, because it grew very naturally next to his pinky finger just as if it was meant to be there. I saw him looking at his hand in satisfaction, curling and uncurling his fingers, but I didn't see anything wrong. At dinner, we sat down to eat our hamburgers together. When he reached for the ketchup bottle, I finally noticed.

"Dad!" I said sharply, dropping my hamburger onto my plate. "What happened to your hand?!"

"Noticed, have you?" he said, grinning.

"You have an extra finger!"

"That's true," he said, grinning even more. He had a handsome face, a narrow straight face with a high forehead and black hair that was beginning to disappear on top. He didn't often remember to get his hair cut, and it usually hung down around his neck and got mixed up with his collar. He had a fiery gleam in his eyes that probably looked slightly insane to people who didn't know him. I liked him best when he was grinning, because a dozen wrinkles would appear on his cheeks out of nowhere, bracketed one within the next like parentheses, and his face would look mischievous.

"It's not a bad match to the other five," he said, holding out his hand for me to see.

"Do you have one on the other hand too?" I asked.

"Nope," he said, holding up both hands for comparison. "Just one, today. But Jem, I bet if you had an extra finger, you wouldn't have dropped your burger like that."

"Dad," I said, making up my mind about it, "it's totally gross."

His eyes opened wide and he looked at me with mingled hurt and astonishment. "What do you mean, *gross*? It's fantastic! Don't you understand?"

I had to admit, it was pretty remarkable. Not too many people could grow an extra finger like that. My dad was a genius; I was sure of that. All the same, I liked to bait him sometimes. I liked to make fun of him just to see his reaction. I didn't want him to get really upset, but I wanted to tease him a little. So I said, "Dad, people aren't *supposed* to have six fingers on their hands."

"Not supposed to. . . . People aren't. . . ," he sputtered, sitting back in his chair and staring at me. Then he leaned forward and began to talk very fast and earnestly. "Jem! How can you say that! Where's your imagination? Do you think Leonardo said, 'gosh, people aren't supposed to fly, so I'll just give the whole thing up'? Do you think he said that? Do you?"

Leonardo da Vinci was my dad's primary hero. Everything came back to Leonardo sooner or later. Dad even had a picture of da Vinci framed over his bed. It was a copy of a charcoal drawing that the artist had done himself, looking into a mirror when he was an old man, and the face was lined and hairy and strange. The eyes were the same as my dad's eyes. Thoughtful, deep, and slightly insane. I used to think it was a picture of my grandfather; and in a sense it was. The spirit of Leonardo had helped to shape my father's mind.

"Everyone else," my father continued, "all those ordinary people with little brains, they said that people weren't supposed to fly. Only birds were supposed to fly. They thought Lenny was crazy. Why would he want to turn himself into a bird? But no. He wasn't crazy. He invented the helicopter. Did you know that?'

"Yes, Dad, actually I did know that," I said, realizing that I had started him up a bit more forcefully than I had intended. But he didn't even hear me. He kept right on going. I was doomed to another dinner lecture on Leonardo, so I picked up my hamburger and decided to make the best of the meal. My dad did have a point. It is not easy to pick up a large juicy burger in a large bun, with lettuce and pickles and tomatoes piled inside precariously. An extra finger might have stabilized it better.

"Everyone else," my father raged, his eyes beginning to bug out, "said he was crazy. But he didn't care. He invented the airplane. Did you know that? And the bicycle. He drew a bicycle in his notebook, gears and all. And the windmill. And the light bulb. Did you know that? Did you know that he—"

I almost dropped my burger again. I had never heard that one before. "The *what*?" I choked. "It can't be. Thomas Edison invented the light bulb."

"Ah ha!" my father said, realizing that he had got to me. It was a game to us, to see if we could spark a reaction out of each other. "So he thought, old Eddie did. But there it is, in one of Leon's notebooks. A drawing of a light bulb. I saw it myself."

"It's impossible," I said. "There wasn't any electricity back then. That was five hundred years ago."

"Well, okay," he admitted. "Maybe it was a drawing

of a bat brain. I think it might have been. But it sure looked a lot like a light bulb. And you can be sure, if he had lived another ten years, he would have invented a nuclear powered spaceship. He was working on it, you know."

"Come on, Dad. He was not."

"The point is," my dad said, "there's no limit to imagination, except the heavy-duty cinder block walls people put around it themselves out of sheer silliness. So *don't* tell me a person's not supposed to have six fingers." He crammed his burger in his mouth and glared at me as he chewed.

The next day his extra finger was only half as long as a normal one. I saw him staring at it anxiously. The day after that, it was gone, and he was quiet and moody for the rest of the week. He obviously saw his experiment as a failure. I didn't ask him about it because I knew he felt bad and I didn't want to make him feel any worse.

After the incident with the finger, nothing very strange happened for another few years. At least, nothing strange that he brought home from work. Probably lots of strange things happened in his secret lab. Then when I was ten years old, Dad came home from work and called out to me while he was taking off his jacket and boots in the front vestibule. It was a snowy day, and he had walked about two blocks from the nearest subway station.

"Jem!" he said cheerfully, banging the snow off his boots. "Don't panic! Don't be afraid! Might be a bit of a shock at first. But you'll get used to it, I'm sure. Can you hear me?"

I came running from my bedroom. I didn't know what he had done to himself. Had he lost a foot for real? Had he grown fingers all over his face? I was worried because I knew that just about any calamity, the kind that would devastate most people, would probably excite him. His voice had so much enthusiasm this time that I expected a major disaster.

I pulled open the door in the kitchen that led to our vestibule, and then I froze. My dad was not there. Filling the vestibule, looming seven feet tall and five feet wide, stood an orangutan, its orange fur standing out all around it like the corona of the sun, a clump of snow on its head, its beady black eyes glaring down at me out of a wide, hairless, wrinkled, hideous gray face. Its lips sneered back, exposing its yellowed fangs, and it said, "What do you think?"

Dad's new look.

2

For an instant I gagged in terror, and then I got control of myself. I thought he was playing our game again and trying to get me to scream in fright. Luckily I had just been eating a very sticky candy bar with a toffee center, and my teeth were stuck together. So I only made a muffled sound in my first surprise. Then I unstuck my teeth and said, "Hi Dad. How was work today?"

"What?" the orangutan said, glaring down at me.

"I said, how was work? Same old, same old? Anything interesting happen?"

"*What?*" the thing said, staggering backward and goggling at me.

I peered at him closely. "You look different, Dad," I said. "Did you get a haircut? It's a definite improvement."

"*Jem!*" he shouted, outraged. "Did I get a *what*? Look at me! Are you *blind*?"

"Come on, Dad," I said, turning away and walking back into the kitchen of our apartment. "I can practically see the zipper on that thing. What are you trying to pull on me?"

The orangutan lunged through the doorway, bounded into the kitchen, and when its feet landed on the floor the entire room shook with a boom and a rattle, and a cabinet door popped open, and six breakfast bowls jumped out and smashed all over the counter top. The thought crossed my mind that an orangutan costume wouldn't make a person that heavy, unless it had cement in the feet. And in that case, my dad would not be able to bound anywhere. He would be straining to shuffle his feet across the floor.

I turned to face him again, a little less certainly. "That's, um, that's a costume, right? I mean you didn't really. . . . Dad, did you really? . . ."

The orangutan sneered again, showing me all its ghastly teeth. It began to make a sucking, grunting noise that sounded like a giant hacksaw cutting off a horse's head. I cowered against the refrigerator at this awful sound, but gradually realized that the thing was laughing.

"Is that what you thought?" the orangutan said. "A costume? No, Jem, no zipper here." It spread out its long arms, spanning the entire room and touching the opposite walls with its knuckles. "It's genuine 100% great ape material."

Now that I was beginning to understand the truth, I started to tremble. "You turned yourself into an orangutan?" I said.

"Very good," he said, sneering at me again. I realized that the sneer was his version of a smile. "You remember your zoology. Yes, that's exactly right, Jem. An orangutan. An especially large one. Obviously the vocal apparatus is modified to allow for the production of human speech, requiring a reshaping of the hyoid process and the. . . ."

"Dad," I said, "is it, like, permanent, or will it go back?"

"Go back?" he said. "You mean, disappear? Turn back into a person? Not this time. No sir. I'm certain. It's absolutely permanent."

"But Dad," I said, and now I began to feel sad. "Can't you go back to your old self?"

"My old self?" he said, scratching his head with an enormous knobby finger. "Why would I want to do that?"

"But," I said, and stopped. I almost said, "People aren't supposed to look like orangutans," but I caught myself in time. I knew better than to try that approach.

He seemed to take my hesitation as a sign that

I still did not quite believe him. Actually, I did. I had no more doubts. Turning himself into an orangutan without first thinking about the consequences was exactly the impulsive sort of thing he would do. "Here, feel it," he said, holding his hand out toward me. "It's for real." I touched his hand, and it was solid and warm and strong. It was a real hand.

"What about the poor animal?" I said.

"Huh?" he said. "What poor animal?"

"Did you get it from a zoo?"

"Jem, don't talk drivel. I generated the plan on a computer. I didn't steal anyone's body. Obviously, if I had taken an actual body, I wouldn't have been able to shape the hyoid process to enable the efficient production of—"

"But," I said, "what will people say? How will you go to work?"

He waved his hand as if brushing away a swarm of irrelevant details. "The point is," he said, and then he paused and grinned again. "Actually, I got some interesting reactions on the subway."

"They let you on the subway?"

"To tell you the truth, I think the subway guard was a little nervous about stopping me. But hey, it's New York, and there's a lot of strange people in the city. Everybody knows that. So I don't think it's a big deal. Jem, I'm starving. What do you say we go out for dinner and celebrate? I know a great vegetarian restaurant a few blocks away. Ah, I feel like a really big salad tonight."

The Landlord was a dried up stick.
I didn't like him.

3

We walked down the street in the snow. It was dark out already and the snow looked very beautiful falling through the cones of light underneath the street lamps. Sometimes people stared at us, and some of them laughed as if they thought it was a joke, but a lot of people didn't even seem to notice. They were too busy shopping or trying to flag down a taxi. I was in my coat and boots, hat and mittens, holding my father's hand. My father, who didn't own any clothes big enough for an orangutan, wore his boots unlaced and a big umbrella to keep the snow from his head. His fur was so long and shaggy that he didn't mind the cold very much. His legs were short in comparison to the rest of his body, and his knees stuck out to the sides, so that at every step his body rocked from side to side.

"Ah, it's such a treat, Jem," he said. "Such a new perspective. I never was so tall before."

"Yes Dad," I said, but not very enthusiastically. I was of two minds about the situation. On the one hand, walking down the street with a giant orangutan had a certain coolness factor. I could imagine my friends from school being seriously jealous, except that none of them lived near us so we were unlikely to meet them. On the other hand, maybe we were a little too sensational. Somebody might call the police on us. One old lady saw us coming, clutched her handbag to her stomach, and scurried down a side street.

We reached the restaurant and opened the door to come in. The waitress saw us and yelped in surprise.

"Um, a table for two," I said.

"Better make it three," my dad said. "I might need two chairs."

When she realized that an orangutan was talking to her, she yelped even louder. She stammered to me to wait for a moment, and then ran to the back of the restaurant.

After a while, the manager came out wearing a very nice white suit. He was calm and professional. "I'm sorry, Son," he said to me. "We don't allow pets in the restaurant."

"I'm not a pet," my father said. "I'm his dad. We'd like a table for three. And your celery special. I feel like celery today."

The man blinked and a stringy muscle in his cheek twitched, but he did not lose his calm. He peered up into my father's face. "I apologize, sir. We never admit patrons who are not properly dressed."

"But I don't own anything big enough," my dad said.

"Then," the manager said, "I suggest you visit a tailor. Good night." And he closed the door in our faces.

"It's discrimination!" my father said on our way back to the apartment. "It's outrageous!"

"Dad," I said, rolling my eyes in annoyance, "what did you *think* would happen?"

That night I walked down the street to the supermarket and bought dinner for the two of us: a microwave dinner for me, and three heads of lettuce, six packages of celery, and four packages of carrots for my father. He grabbed hold of our kitchen cleaver and in three seconds chopped up the vegetables into bite sizes and tossed them down his mouth, smacking his lips and gulping and burping.

"Sorry," he said, with a smirk. "That's the way orangutans do it."

"That's okay," I said, grinning back at him. "I don't mind."

I felt more comfortable than I had a few hours ago. I was beginning to see my dad's facial expressions in this big hairy creature. It really was him. Inside, he hadn't changed at all. If he wanted to look like a giant carpet, I could deal. My friend Joey's father had a wart on his nose so big it was actually bigger than his nose; and my friend Ken's father had a very long neck with folds and wrinkles like a turkey. You could see the folds jiggling whenever he talked. My dad, in present form, looked a lot better than that. Besides, geniuses do funny things sometimes. Whatever made him happy. Whatever floated his boat. All this homespun philosophy, I began to notice, didn't entirely take away my anxiety. I was still worried about our future, because even if I had come more or less to terms with his enlarged and hairy condition, I didn't know how other people might react. If they all reacted like the people in the restaurant, then we were in for some trouble.

The next day was a vacation day for me and I stayed home from school. My father went to work as usual at six o'clock. Most days he didn't come home until evening, but this day he stomped in the front door in the late morning, his long shaggy arms wrapped around two large cardboard boxes full of papers. He dumped the boxes on the kitchen table and turned to me.

"Well," he said, in a grim voice, "I quit my job."

"You *what*?"

"Yes, I quit. I had enough. I told him so. I said it right out. I didn't pussyfoot my words. Well, to be honest, I got fired at the same time that I quit. I mean, I shouted 'I quit!' just as my boss was shouting, 'You're fired!' and you'd have to check the video to see who said what first. I think I was first. But he was mighty quick on the draw, so I don't know. Photo finish, as they say. In any case, it all comes down to the same thing." He pulled out a chair and sat, his enormous hairy bottom sagging off of the sides of the chair. He put his elbows on the table and his head in his hands, and looked at me gloomily.

"How come you quit?" I said, sitting down on the other side of the table and looking at him between the boxes of papers.

"Well, okay, it was like this. I had no trouble getting into the center. I have a card key, and the card reader doesn't care what you look like so long as you have your card. I had just sat down and started on my work, when Clapton comes in and says, 'Hi Carl,' and he doesn't think anything of it. And Snupplee he comes in and says, 'Hi Carl,' and goes right to work at *his* desk. Everything is just fine. Then after a while, Old Gordon Spork calls me into his office. And he says, 'Carl, have a seat,' and I knew that was a bad sign. Especially since I broke the chair sitting in it. 'Carl,' he says, 'this kind of thing has gone on too long. It's got to stop. We really loved your acid bomb, but—' "

"You built an acid bomb?" I said.

"Sure," my dad said. "Not on purpose. It was kind of an accidental side effect, and not my main line of research."

I was fascinated. I had never heard him talk so much about his work before. I didn't even know any of the people he had just mentioned. "Isn't it all supposed to be secret?" I said eagerly.

"Sure," he said. "But I don't work for them anymore, so I don't care. We built an acid bomb. And the government loved it. They like anything that can melt people. They gave us a list of priorities a few years ago, and melting was up there with mangling, smashing, and boiling. Ugh. I tell you. But do they care for a really useful thing like this?" He pointed to his hairy chest. "Do they? Do you think they care?"

"Dad," I said, "not to be negative, and I'm not criticizing, but what's actually useful about it?"

My dad did a double take and looked at me. "That's odd, that's what old Spork said. I told him, 'Come on, it's right up you're alley. It's a disguise. It's camouflage. Supposing a spy needs to go somewhere incognito.' "

"Um," I said, "are you sure that being an orangutan would make the spy blend in better?"

"Ha!" my father said. He was getting agitated now, and he jumped to his feet and began pacing the room with a Boom Boom every time his foot hit the ground. I could hear the dishes rattling in the cabinets but none of them flew out and broke this time. "Ha! Spork said that, too! That smarmy old fool he says, 'Well Carl, you sure blend in great. I bet nobody noticed a nine foot gorilla on the subway this morning, reading the New York Times.' But, I mean, come on. First of all, I'm not a gorilla. And second, supposing a government spy needed to mingle with a society of subversive orangutans and get information from them? It could happen, right? And it'd be great for the witness protection program, too. But he didn't see any of it. He just couldn't see the utility of it. Some people have no imagination."

"It's okay dad," I said. I was getting a little alarmed at his agitation. I didn't want him to accidentally break our kitchen table now that he was so much stronger than he used to be. "Calm down. It's the government's loss, if they're too silly to understand."

"That's exactly right, Jem!" he shouted, getting even more agitated. "You're right! That's what I thought, too. I said, 'Spork,' I said, 'this is the crowning achievement of twenty years of work! Everything I've done here has led up to this! And if you don't appreciate it, then I QUIT!' And that's when he yelled, 'You're FIRED!' at the same time. But it might have had to do with my foot accidentally going through the wall into the next guy's office."

"What will we do now?" I said.

"Now?" he said. "Oh, we're okay. They let me take home all my important papers. All they cared about was that idiot acid bomb, and they couldn't care less about my real work. It's all here. I've already got the next project planned out." He waved his huge hand at the boxes on the table. Peering into the nearest one, I saw a messy pile of drawings and scribbles. They looked like reproductions of Leonardo's notebook pages. "That's right," he said, bounding over to the table and beginning to paw through the box. "It's all here, Jem. I've been re-reading Folio 217A and I think that—"

"But Dad," I said, "can you even get another job? I mean, what about an income, and that kind of thing?"

"An *income*?" he said, jumping backwards and staring at me, his hand cupped on his shaggy forehead. "I hadn't thought of that. Good point. I suppose I can work at a gas station. My arms are so long, I could squeegee both sides of the windshield without walking around the car. Ha! Well, anyway, I was saying. . . ."

Just then the doorbell rang. Whoever was outside

our apartment was very impatient and banged and kicked and kept up a racket, until my dad and I ran to the vestibule and yanked open the door.

Our landlord was standing in the corridor outside. He was a very small man, a thin and wrinkly man who looked like he had lived his life with so little humor that he had dried up into a kind of stick. His face was always sour, and it was especially sour now. "What's going on here?" he shouted at me, since I had gotten to the door first. "The people under you think the ceiling's about to cave in!"

"Sorry," I said. "It's just my dad jumping around. His feet are kind of—"

"Good God!" the landlord shouted, looking past me at my dad. "What's that? No pets allowed! It's in the lease! What's a great filthy brute like that doing in one of my apartments?!"

"What do you mean, a filthy brute?" my dad said. He was already worked up about leaving his job, and I could see he was in an argumentative mood. "Who are you calling a brute?"

"It can *talk*?" the landlord shouted, bits of spit flying from his mouth in his agitation. "You got a circus ape in my building, and it's jumping around knocking the lights off the ceiling below! How dare you!"

"That's offensive and bigoted," my dad shouted

back, and his larger chest cavity gave him a huge voice that easily overpowered the landlord's. "I'm your tenant."

"You're Carl Martin?" the landlord said. "You look different. What the heck do you look like that for?"

"It's none of your business," my dad said. "It's a free country. I can turn myself into an orangutan if I want to. It's a lifestyle choice."

"A life style choice!" the landlord shrieked, his little body swelling up with rage. "A life style choice! Let me tell you where to put your lifestyle choice! I'm a moral man and I don't allow lifestyle choices! It's disgusting! I want you out of here. I know my rights! I'm giving you one week before I put a lock on the door and sell everything you own. I'm evicting you! I won't have a filthy animal living in my building!"

He stormed out, and as he stomped away down the corridor I shouted after him, "My dad is not filthy, you filthy old dried up stick!" I was really angry.

We put everything we could in the wagon.

4

My dad staggered back into the kitchen and sank down into a chair. He put his face in his hands and groaned. "We're ruined!" he said. "What's wrong with these people? How can they all be so *dull*? If Leo ever saw a talking orangutan, do you think he'd have reacted like that? Do you? He'd have whipped out a notebook and sketched it! He'd have asked how he could get the same way himself."

"It's okay, Dad," I said, putting my hand on his furry shoulder. "We'll just go somewhere else." I didn't like to see him upset, so I tried to sound cheerful. But I thought that our problems were probably just beginning. "Dad," I said, "is it too late to go make up with your boss, and get your job back, and turn yourself into a person again?"

"Not a chance," he said. "It would take another ten years of research to get the reverse transformation.

And what's the excitement in that? It's boring. It's a re-tread. Anyway, the point is, old Spork is an idiot with a squishy tomato for a brain, and I'm not going back there for anything. No, you're right Jem, we'll just have to go somewhere else and make do the best we can."

Making do turned out to be difficult. My dad tried to rent another apartment, but when he showed up at a realtor's office they panicked and shooed him out the door. He sent me instead, but I was so young that they didn't take me seriously. He tried to get a job, and he did pretty well over the telephone, but every time he showed up for an interview he got rejected. Not even a gas station would hire him. He came very close at one body shop, showing off his long arms and explaining about the squeegee. The mechanics who worked there were impressed, but the boss thought it was too risky. "Fact is," the boss said, "it's against regulations. Sure, I could do with a big monkey to lift the engines onto the service rack, but what do you think the inspectors'd say if they saw me working a monkey? It's illegal. It's cruelty. I'd get shut down. Sorry, no can do." He even tried to get a job at the Bronx Zoo, because he thought they might have a use for someone in his condition. But that was the biggest disaster of all. He almost got shot with a tranquilizer dart when he knocked at the zoo's front office, and he had to run home double quick to escape the zookeepers.

Everything was a no go, and our final week was disappearing from under us. On the evening before the eviction, my dad and I sat at the kitchen table eating our last supper and trying to figure out what to do. We were desperate.

"I could buy a tent," I said, "and we could camp in Central Park."

"It's twenty below!" my dad said. "It's snowing like crazy! We can't camp out, we'd freeze to death." He tossed a quarter of a head of cabbage into his mouth and swallowed it whole.

"Mountain climbers do it all the time," I said, dipping a chicken finger in mustard sauce and eating it. "They get the right equipment, and they go camping out on the top of Mount Everest for weeks at a time and cook food over a gas fire, and it's real fun. Dad, what else can we do?"

"You got me," he said. "You sure got me there. Maybe that's all we can do. We can travel up the state, camping as we go."

Right away I began to feel better. The disaster didn't seem so disastrous suddenly. It seemed like we could have a lot of fun; and I wouldn't have to go to school, of course. "I bet EMS is still open," I said eagerly. "They have a Christmas sale. I could go right now and get supplies. Give me your credit card, Dad, and I'll go do it!"

I could see him thinking hard about it, chewing on an apple or two that he had put whole into his mouth. The more he thought about it, the less worried he looked. All week he had looked anxious, and his gray leathery face had folded up into wrinkles around the eyes, and now I saw the wrinkles smoothing out. Finally he produced a gigantic belch that made the long hairs around his mouth whiffle in a breeze, and he looked at me and said, "Jem, you're right. That's the only thing we can do. After a while, after we travel around, maybe we'll find somewhere nice and settle down. But you better go quick before they close!" He knew he couldn't go with me, because he couldn't go into a store without inciting a riot.

Here is what I bought: A six-man mountaineering tent. I figured my dad was about the size of five and a half men, and I made up the other half. Two kerosene stoves. Six canisters of kerosene. A deluxe artic survival suit for a small person about my size. It was the kind of suit that you inflated with an air pump, and it bulged out around you and kept you warm even if you got dipped in liquid nitrogen. The picture on the tag showed two people, one of them in a deluxe arctic survival suit and one of them in an ordinary suit, both of them being dipped in liquid nitrogen. The survival suit guy came out smiling, and the other guy came out crunchy. None of the suits would have fit my dad, so I bought a deluxe artic survival quilt that I figured he could wrap around himself if he needed it. Special snow traction boots for both of us. A hammer for hammering in the tent pegs. Rope to tie our supplies together. And an enormous metal wagon, about ten feet long and five feet wide, to put everything in. The store clerks were happy because they made a great sale. I was a good customer, so they didn't worry that I was only a kid. I told them that my father was a mountain climber and I was buying supplies for an expedition we were going on together. Which was exactly the truth. The whole lot was incredibly expensive, but we didn't have a problem with money. My dad had lots of money in his bank account.

I had to drag that wagon all the way home, and it nearly dislocated my arms it was so heavy. I couldn't bring it inside, and I couldn't leave it on the sidewalk outside because a lot of people in New York would have liked to nick that tent. It was a nice tent. So I rang our bell and waited for my dad to come out. He was very excited when he saw all the things I had bought. I could tell that the spark of adventure had gotten into him, and he wasn't gloomy anymore. He was his usual self again.

"Jem, it's fantastic!" he said, throwing his arms up over his head and laughing. "It's perfect! You did a great job. That wagon's big enough to fit a lot more stuff. I'll go bring down the important things, and we'll have to leave the rest behind. You wait here."

He brought down his two boxes of da Vinci papers, and two kitchen chairs, and the kitchen table, and a wooden drawer full of drinking glasses and plates and forks and knives and things like that, and piles of clothes and pillows and blankets, and a radio, and the salt and pepper shakers, and sixty-seven books from the library, and cooking pans, and an electric fan in case we ever got too hot somewhere that had an electric outlet, and a blender that was broken but he thought maybe he could fix someday, and a nice wooden bird feeder that had never been used and was still in its package, and a box of powdered laundry detergent so we could wash our clothes, and a big plastic garbage can to wash our clothes in, and toilet paper and bath towels and shampoo, and the shower curtain, even though it was getting a little yellow from soap, but it might come in handy if we ever settled down somewhere nice, and last of all, carried delicately all by itself, his framed picture of Leonardo as an old man, all hairy and lined and with slightly crazy eyes, wrapped up in plastic food wrap to keep out the damp.

I had never seen my dad at work before. Even though his hands were three times larger than a normal person's, they zipped around here and there at high speed and it seemed like he had about a million fingers. He tied everything together with ropes and made it fit into the wagon neat and square like a puzzle. Then he tied our tent fabric over the top of the pile to keep off the snow. He was done in a minute and a half. The wagon was stacked up about ten feet tall, taller than he was, and I was worried at first that it was too heavy. But he grabbed hold of the handle and tugged, and wheeled it along the sidewalk just fine. He didn't seem to notice the weight. It was nothing to him. Maybe he could have lifted up the whole thing in his arms if he had wanted to.

I walked beside him. I was happy now, and so was he. Somebody said, "Hey, look at all those Christmas presents those people bought!" and a little girl pulled on her mother's sleeve and said, "Mummy, is that a real monkey?" and her mother hushed her up and said, "Don't point, Spongella, it's rude," and a little boy turned to his daddy and said, "Hey Pop! Look at the funny Santa!" And the truth was, my dad *was* like Santa, and our wagon *was* piled up with Christmas toys, because we were starting out on the most exciting adventure I could imagine. And if that wasn't Christmas, I didn't know what was.

"Where do we go first, Dad?" I said.

"Well, Jem," my father said, "what say we turn left up there at 34th and hit Starbucks?"

That's what we did. My dad waited outside with the wagon and I bought us three large steaming hot chocolates, one for me and two for him. My dad couldn't digest milk very well anymore, so I had to get two Soy No Whip Hot Chocs for him. Then we sat on the curb next to the wagon and drank our hot chocolates under the lamp light, with snow falling on our heads. My dad gave a huge loud slurp at the drink in his right hand, and then a slurp at the drink in his left hand, his lips vibrating against each other, and then he leaned back against the side of our wagon and said, "Ahhhhh, Jem, this is the life. I tell you. Who would have thought it, two weeks ago? Goes to show, doesn't it?"

Hot chocolate.

5

"We might have a long night of walking, Jem," my dad said, sipping at his chocolate. "We should try to get out of the city as fast as possible. I don't like the way people keep looking at us. Once we get into the countryside we can go easier."

"Are we going anywhere in particular?" I askcd.

"That's an important question," my dad said. "I want to head north of the city and explore around. It's important for my next project."

"Uh oh," I said. "I hope you're not going to turn *me* into anything."

"Don't be silly. I hope I'm turning you into a creative and imaginative person. The next project will be a wonderful and amazing adventure, Jem. I always wanted to visit the final resting place of Leonardo."

"You want to drag our wagon to Italy? Won't the Atlantic be hard to get over?"

"Very clever, smarty. He didn't die in Italy. He died in America."

"Dad! He died in Amboise in 1519."

"Jem, you're amazing. You remember me telling you that?"

"You only told me about thirty times," I muttered.

"Oh, ha ha. The truth is, Jem, I've been studying notebook 217A, and I think he staged his own death in Amboise, and came over to America. Here, look. . . ."

He slid his foot out of his boot to take hold of one of his drinks. The toes on his feet, of course, were flexible and almost as good as fingers. Then with his free hand he reached behind him into the wagon and rummaged in one of the boxes of papers, which he had packed conveniently close to the edge in case a sudden inspiration came over him.

"Look." He smoothed a piece of paper on his lap. It was a photocopied page of one of Leonardo's notebooks. "Plain as plain. Can't you see? Look at that line scribbled in the corner."

"I can't read it," I said.

"Of course you can't," he said. "It's mirror writing. He always wrote in mirror writing. Bizarre, isn't it? If he was alive today, how fast do you think he'd get fired from his job? Here, I always keep a mirror handy." He rummaged in the box again and took out a little vanity mirror. "Now take a look."

"Sorry, still can't read it."

"Well sure," he said. "It's in Italian. But I never go anywhere without my Italian English dictionary. Let's translate the thing word for—"

"Dad, just tell me what it says."

"Right. It says, 'A farmer, who looks just like me, has died and his body has been brought to me for anatomical studies. In my examination of this body,' get this Jem, he says, 'In my examination of this body, the amazing coincidence of similarity has brought to my mind a new plan.' That's all he says. But what else could the plan be? It's perfectly clear. He staged his death. He propped the farmer up at his desk, dressed him up in his clothes, his hat on his head and his pencil in the man's hand, shoved a carrot stick down the man's windpipe, just to make the thing look plausible, and then snuck out the back door. That's what happened. I'm telling you. He was only sixty-seven. He had ten more years in him, at least."

"I can see your point," I said, "but Dad, it seems like kind of a stretch. Maybe he only meant to play a joke on a friend. Maybe that was the plan. Was he into practical jokes a lot? Because he might have—"

"Jem! Practical jokes? Lenny? You think he had time to worry about practical jokes? He was too busy trying to figure out how the world worked. I'm telling you. He saw his chance and got out of dodge.

He went sight-seeing. And he filled up another fifty notebooks that nobody's found yet."

"Well," I said skeptically, "it's interesting all right, but, to be honest, it's not a lot to go on."

"It isn't," my dad admitted. "And a year ago when I read that sentence, I didn't think too much about it. I filed it in the back of my mind. I decided it probably meant nothing. But it had a way of coming back to me now and then, when I was going to sleep at night. I'd gaze up at his picture. 'Leonard,' I'd say to him, 'Leonard, what—' "

"Okay Dad, I get the idea. You found something else in the meantime."

"That's exactly right. Last month I found this." He rummaged around in the box again and took out a stack of papers, photocopies of what must have been an old and crumbling book. "Now!" he said, slapping the papers onto the curb between us. "Take a look at *that* and see how far your practical joke gets you. Huh?"

"Is that in his mirror writing too?"

"Mirror writing? No! It's Spanish. It's a ship's log. The Santa Torpedo. It sailed from Spain in 1519, the year that Leonardo died. Or pretended to die. Spooky coincidence, isn't it? Look. A list of the sailors, with a brief description of each one. Notice this fellow. 'Old but immensely strong Italian.'

That's the description. His name? 'Leonardo Vince.' What do you think of that, Jem?"

I began to see what he meant. A prickle went down my spine. I couldn't read Spanish, but I could read the name all right. "You think he signed on as a sailor?"

"Of course he did. He wanted to see the world from a new perspective. His mind was wide open, I tell you. The Santa Torpedo landed just north of Manhattan Island. It wasn't called that at the time, of course. I've only just started to translate the log, but I expect there's a lot more information in it. Jem, we're going to explore around, do some detective work, and track down Leonardo's final resting place. We're going to hunt for his last notebook."

"Dad," I said, "I like it. I do! I think we should start right away. Especially since it's, um, getting kind of cold here on the curb."

We drained the last of our hot chocolates into our gullets, Dad pulled his boot back on his foot, and we set out on our journey, Dad pulling the wagon, rolling side to side because of his orangutan gait, me striding along beside him, the snow sifting down around us, and the city gradually falling as quiet as it ever gets at night. To tell the truth, I didn't believe a word about Leonardo in America. I thought it was just my dad being nutty. But a quest is a quest, and I was as happy as a ten-year-old boy could be.

Into the snow.

6

We walked and we walked. At first we sang Christmas carols together, my dad taking the base notes beautifully. But my throat got chilled from the cold air and I had to wrap a scarf around my face, which put an end to the singing. Then we trudged in silence, one step after the next, the wind in our faces or hitting us from behind depending on the way it was channeled by the buildings around us. The snow kept falling, and after a few hours it was as deep as my ankles. My dad didn't mind the snow, but I found it exhausting to walk through, so he picked me up and put me on top of the wagon. I took a rest up there sitting ten feet off the street, my legs dangling over the front. The wind was stronger up above, but I was wrapped up in my arctic survival suit and I didn't mind it, except on my hands and face. It did blow right through the knitting of my scarf.

After a while my dad made a harness out of some extra rope and harnessed himself to the front of the wagon, so that he could walk more easily and swing his long arms. Sometimes he even went on all fours, just for a change. He didn't seem to feel the weight at all, and I held up an umbrella to keep the snow from his head.

We traveled all night. Sometimes I came down and walked beside my dad, to warm up my legs, and sometimes I perched on top to take a rest. Around two in the morning the snow stopped and the sky cleared up. I lay on my back on top of our pile, and I could see the stars up above me very bright and very deep, and my breath rising up in puffs. I wasn't used to seeing stars, because the city lights tend to out-glare them. But we were outside the city already and walking along a dark back road. It was nice to feel the vibration of the wagon under me and listen to Dad's footsteps in the snow and to his enormous breathing. After a while I felt so comfortable that I dozed.

When my dad woke me, we were in the middle of nowhere on the side of a road and it was seven in the morning. I sat up and a load of snow slid off of my arctic suit. The snow had started falling again. It was coming down fast, and everything was covered in gray. The bushes on either side were humps and the road was just a kind of long depression softened with snow. You couldn't tell if it was a paved road or a backcountry gravel road. It didn't have any streetlights; the only light came from the sun that was lost somewhere up above the snow clouds. In the gray light, I could see our wagon tracks trailing back along the road until they disappeared to sight, but I didn't see any other tracks. We must have been the only ones to travel along that road in the past hour. My dad helped me down and we stood by the side of the wagon.

"We did pretty well," my dad said, checking his watch. "I bet we made thirty miles. But I can't go anymore; I need a break."

"You should have stopped sooner Dad," I said. "You must be frozen."

"It's sweaty work pulling that thing," he said. "Now that we've stopped, though, the sweat is beginning to freeze on me. Ugh! Let's get off the road and make camp."

Dad pulled our wagon behind some bushes and low trees that were banked with snow. He didn't know if it was legal to camp on the side of a public road, and so he thought it was better to keep out of view. Also, the bushes gave us some shelter from the wind.

I wasn't much use. I couldn't do much except stand

nearby and keep my mittens over my nose to stop it from freezing and falling off. My dad was astonishing to watch. He was getting used to his new shape, I think, and he took off his boots and set in with all four endings so to speak, both hands and both feet. He flew over our wagonload, undid the ropes, unpacked everything, and in about four minutes he had built a shelter for us. He used the kitchen table on its side for one wall, the wagon on its side for another wall, and the artic survival quilt, and the tent, and some blankets, for the roof, and made what was practically a cabin. I could stand up in the center, but my dad had to go on all fours because he was so tall. He fixed down the sides by filling our plastic garbage can with snow, packing it in hard, and then upending the can, so that a big solid cylinder of snow came out. With those cylinders as building blocks all around us, we had pretty good protection from the wind.

Inside, he lay the shower curtain down as a floor, and set up our chairs, and turned the wooden drawer upside down as a table, and placed some candles on the table to give us light, but he said we had to be careful not to knock over the candles or we'd catch on fire. Then we ate dinner. Or breakfast, I suppose. I had a bologna and mustard sandwich. Dad had an entire sack of raw sweet potatoes, and some strawberries. The strawberries were frozen, but he didn't mind. He said they were like a frozen dessert. We also melted some snow in a pot to drink. By that time, the inside of our tent had warmed up from the candles and from our own body heat. I had to take off my arctic coat, I got so hot, and I sat around in a sweater with the sleeves rolled up to the elbows.

"Take a look outside, Jem," Dad said, so I untied the flap and stuck my head out. All I could see was gray. The air was full of snow going all directions and I couldn't see more than about two yards from our front door. I got chilled from ten seconds of looking, and I had to duck back inside and tie the flap closed again.

"It's a real snow storm," I said, brushing the flakes off the top of my head. I wasn't worried at all, because we were snug in our tent. I was happy. I couldn't remember the last time I had had so much fun. "How long do you think it'll last?"

"No telling," my dad said. "But I feel like I could sleep for about three days, Jem. Maybe it'll be over by the time I wake up." He rolled up in his blankets, his face to the wall, and started snoring right away. He had a soft snore, but it was also a very low, rumbly snore, and it set the whole tent vibrating. That and the wind outside were the only sounds. I was used to a city life with traffic and sirens and shouting, and this rising and falling sound of the wind made me feel lonesome.

I couldn't sleep. I had had an easy night, comparatively, and I had also slept for a few hours before dawn. Now I sat cross-legged on the floor beside our makeshift table and started to look through Dad's boxes of papers. I didn't have anything else to do. On top of one box I saw the photocopied pages of the ship's log, written in Spanish. And when I dug around in the box, I found a Spanish-English dictionary. I didn't know how far Dad had gotten in translating the log, but I thought I could give it a try, at least until I felt sleepy. So I found a pencil, and some blank paper to write down my translation, and I got started. I opened up a bag of celery and munched on a stick now and then. Now that my dad was an orangutan, I was eating less junk food and more veggies, which was probably healthy.

Flipping through the pages, I noticed a list of names at the very end of the log. It was a roster of all the sailors who had disembarked in Spain at the end of the voyage, and of how much each one had been paid. Leonardo Vince was not on the list. Somewhere between the time the Santa Torpedo had left the coast of Spain for America, and the time it had returned, he had disappeared.

I decided to start at the beginning of the log and

work my way through it. I didn't have to translate every word. Usually after the first few words of an entry, I could tell that it had nothing to do with Leonardo. Every little thing had been written down. All the spare canvas, all the spare wood for repairs, the food, the cloth, the number of chickens in the chicken coop on the deck, the number of pigs down below, the bottles of wine for the captain, it was all spelled out. Whoever wrote that log seemed to be interested mainly in how much everything cost.

Still, I began to get a sense of what it was like on that ship. And with the wind roaring over the tent, whistling in the ropes, I had fun pretending that I was right there on board. I knew what the sailors ate every day, and I knew how fast the ship went, and whether the water was stormy or calm. I saw a word that translated as "overboard," and I got worried about Leonardo. It would be a horrible waste if the great man simply fell over the side one day. Also, our journey to his final resting place would end up uncomfortably watery. But when I translated the whole entry, I found out that it was one of the chickens that went overboard. The cook had been about to cut its head off on the railing, when a gust of wind ripped the chicken out of the cook's hands and tossed it into the ocean. At first I felt sorry for the chicken, but then I decided that a chicken stood a better chance in the Atlantic Ocean than in a cook's pot.

I skimmed along, munching celery sticks as I worked, translating a word here and a phrase there to get a sense of what was happening on deck. A few hours later and about a quarter of the way through the log, I ran into an entry that was so interesting I put my celery stick down on the table and translated the passage very carefully, word for word. It went like this: "Six good iron rods ruined. One of the men caught entertaining the aft cabin by bending them with his bare hands. When ordered to do so, couldn't bend them back perfectly straight. Denied rations that evening as punishment." I remembered that when Leonardo was a boy, he used to do the same trick with iron rods to impress his friends.

Until that moment, I had been doubtful about my dad's theory. I could see a lot of coincidences stacking up, but I wasn't sure that the Leonardo Vince on that ship was really the same as Leonardo da Vinci. Now I felt more certain. Who else would do such a thing? And poor Leonardo, sent to his bed without dinner. I felt sorry for him. He was only trying to amuse the other sailors. I thought about waking up my dad and showing him the passage, but he was still sound asleep snoring on the other side of the tent. I figured I could tell him later; there was no hurry.

I turned back to the manuscript and continued to skim through the entries, but for a long time I didn't find anything else interesting. No mention of the Italian sailor. Finally I found the part where the ship reached land. I didn't understand the nautical notation, but I guessed that my father had deciphered the numbers. He already knew that the ship had landed just north of Manhattan. The first day after the ship reached America, a group of six men rowed ashore, explored a little bit, shot some deer and a squirrel for food, and rowed back to the ship. The next day they sailed a mile down the coast and tried again. They were looking for a river or a stream, so they could fill up their water casks with fresh water.

The entry for the third day of land exploration went like this: "V. of shore party, disappeared into forest, not seen again. Men searched two hours, no sign. Captain's opinion, jumped ship. First Mate's opinion, killed by ferocious animal. Will wait two days."

Two days later, according to the log, the Santa Torpedo upped anchor and sailed to a new location on the coast. Vince was never mentioned again. I skimmed through the rest of the log and didn't find his name anywhere. Whoever wrote the log seemed to care more about the hides of the strange animals they had shot and the prices they might be able to get back in Spain.

"Dad!" I said. I couldn't help it. I had to tell him. "Dad, quick, wake up and look!"

"What?!" he shouted, sitting up and bashing his head on the roof of the tent. He was under the artic quilt part of the roof, so I don't think it hurt him any. "Where's the tiger?" He looked around wildly.

"No tiger, Dad," I said. "Wake up and look."

His hair stood out around his head and his eyes were stretched wide open so that, even as an orangutan, he looked insane. "What's wrong?" he shouted.

"Nothing's wrong, Dad. Did you ever read through this ship's log?"

As soon as I mentioned the ship's log, and waved it around in the light, he woke up thoroughly and scrambled across the tent on all fours to take a look. "I only got to a part of it here and there. Did you find anything, Jem?"

"Listen to this, Dad." I read the part about the iron rods.

"That's him!" my dad sang out. "That's got to be him!"

Then I read the part about disappearing into the forest. When I was done reading, Dad said in a hushed voice, "You found it, Jem. That's the critical entry. By God, he jumped ship, and he disappeared in the New World. Now we have something to go on!"

"But don't you think he might have gotten eaten?" I said.

"Nonsense!" Dad said. "He probably had a knife and one of those iron rods down his pants. Any bear came around to bother him, and wang! He probably mashed it over the head and then pulled out a notebook to sketch the thing."

"But they didn't find any trace of him," I said. "They didn't even find any trail to follow."

"That's exactly right," my dad said. "Don't you see? If he had been eaten, they would have found a skeleton. That captain was smart. He knew. He knew that Vince had left on purpose. That was Leo's plan to begin with, don't you see? He wanted to explore a new continent. He didn't mean to come back."

"What if he got captured by Indians?" I said.

"He might have," my dad said, thoughtfully. "He might have fallen in with a local tribe. That's very smart, Jem. We'll have to research Native American lore." But then he stopped and smiled at me. "Jem. Listen. Do you hear anything?"

We were quiet a moment. "Nope. What is it, Dad?"

He grinned again. "The wind is gone. And look at the light."

I realized suddenly that the tent was glowing from sunlight that filtered in through the nylon material.

Our candle had gone out a long time ago, but I hadn't noticed. The ship's log had been too absorbing. And the package of celery was empty. I had eaten it all. I hoped it wouldn't give me a stomachache. "What time is it?" I said.

Dad checked his watch, pushing aside the matted hair on his wrist that covered up the dial. "It's five in the afternoon. We've been here all day, and the storm is over. Jem, you better duck outside and see what's happened to the world."

His head looked like a pumpkin,
but he was friendly.

7

The Earth had turned a sparkly white. The sky was clear blue and the sun was bright near the horizon. The bushes were no longer visible; they were bulges of whiteness glittering in the sunlight. They had funny irregular shapes, and reminded me of bears and dinosaurs that had crouched down and gotten covered up. The trees were also covered with snow, but I could still see their dark prickly branches sticking out here and there. The road was a shallow white trench and the wooden telephone poles standing along the road were crusted with white on one side where the wind had blown the hardest. Even the wires that connected the telephone poles had snow on them, and they stood out against the sky as lines of icy white. Everything was absolutely still. The wind had stopped entirely. The air was clear and cold, but not so cold that it hurt my nose or stung my throat. I could put down my hood and look around and enjoy the sight. You can't enjoy the world as much if you are wearing a hood, because it puts a frame around the world and makes you feel like you are watching a television screen; and also it blocks the sound from your ears and makes everything seem unreal. But once I put my hood down, the whole snowy countryside came rushing up around me.

I walked knee deep to the roadside and looked up and down and all directions, but I couldn't see a house or a barn anywhere. All I saw was open fields and snow-covered woods. I saw a few bird tracks in the snow, and some other tracks that I couldn't recognize; but nothing very big, and nothing that wore a boot or a shoe. After a while I started to hear a rumbling sound to my left, and I peered down the road as far as I could. The road bent out of sight about half a mile away, and something came scraping and grinding around the bend into view. It was a snowplow. I thought I would watch it go by and wave at it. It came grinding up slowly, pushing the snow to one side in a huge stack. When it got closer I could see it was not a very high-end snowplow. It was somebody's old rusty pickup truck with a plow blade fixed to the front. I didn't want it to accidentally plow me under, so I stood pretty far back from the roadside and waved as it drove past.

The truck stopped and the window opened. A head stuck out of the window and looked at me. It was a very large, round head, wider than it was tall because the cheeks were so fat, with smile lines around the eyes and the mouth, and with a lot of shaggy blonde hair on top. The face was red, like a giant round pumpkin that somebody had put a wig on. I couldn't tell at first if it was a man or a woman, but when it started to talk I realized it was a man.

"My goodness you sure gave me a fright!" he said. He opened his mouth and his eyes very wide, and laughed very loud, as if he had said something funny. He didn't wait for me to reply, but kept on talking. "I says to myself, 'what is that, is that a bear?' I says, 'Goodness,' I says, 'I'm'a go back and tell Gladys I saw a bear standing on the side of the road,' except if it was a stump or I don't know what, then I thought it was a person. What *are* you doing here all alone on the side of the road? I saw a raccoon about six miles back, poor thing was so froze up and hungry it just sat there and didn't budge, I says, 'If I had a sandwich,' I says to myself, 'I'd toss it out the window for the poor thing,' that's how hungry it looked. Only I wouldn't tell nobody else about it. People like to hunt them. But I didn't expect a bear. I tell you. Then I says to myself, 'Well, Bill, since when is a bear bright blue with red trim?'

Because that's the color of your coat you know. I says, 'That can't be a bear.' I says—"

"Um," I said; I didn't like to interrupt, but I wasn't sure if I'd get the chance otherwise. "Is it very far to the next town?"

"The next town!" the person said. "Depends on what you call a town. There's Sutton, but it's hardly a town at all. And there's Collingwood, which has a nice store which is called Collingwood's and has garden gnomes and things like that which are very nice, you know, made out of stone, and there's . . . say, how long have you been out here, Sonny? You all alone? Did I tell you, you sure give me a fright? I thought you was a bear! You want a ride anywhere?"

"Um," I said, trying to decide which question to answer first, "I'm with my dad."

Bill turned his round head one way and the other, looking everywhere, and said, "I don't see your dad. What is he, froze under the snow?"

"He's in our tent, back there," I said. "We're looking for Indian relics," I added.

He looked surprised and scratched at his nose with a pudgy red hand. "Tell you the truth, it's not such a great time to look for Indian relics. I heard of arrowheads and things like that scattered here and there, but with the snow and all, it's a little hard to spot them. Say, what did you say your name was? Anyways there's Blackwood too. Did I mention Blackwood? That's a town that's got an auction house I got me a radio for six dollars and a broken pair of pliers. Didn't know the darn thing was broke. Well I says to Stan who was next to me, 'Stan,' I says, 'that whole box that's going for fifty cents is got a pair of pliers worth five dollars in it so I'm'a bid on it.' And Stan he says—"

"Um," I said, getting an idea, "is there a town with an Indian museum?"

"Shore!" he said. "There shore is. It's about thirty, thirty-five miles up the road, it's called Stockton and that museum has a lot of books and old pictures and arrows and things like that, very pretty, I took my son there once, he's more interested in other things, he says, 'Dad,' he says, 'they got a museum for Power Rangers?' Can you beat that? That's what he says!" The man opened his eyes and his mouth again and laughed hard at me. I thought he was a very jolly person, but a little hard to talk to.

Then his face changed and his hair seemed to stand up on his head. He stared over my shoulder and said, "By God, kid, you better jump in the truck as fast as you can, there's a bear behind you. It et your dad, I'm afraid. Hop in quick, before it eats you too!"

"That *is* my dad," I said. I looked over my shoulder

just to make sure, because I didn't want to get eaten by a bear. Sure enough, my dad was climbing out of the tent hole, and a load of snow had fallen in his eyes and he was staggering around trying to brush it out.

I had a clever idea. I stepped up to the truck and said in a low voice, "My dad's an Indian. I mean, a Native American. He's an elder in the, um, Otchig tribe. That's his ceremonial outfit. He's real nice, you'll like him. But don't mention to him that I told you about his tribe, because he doesn't like to talk about it."

"Ah ha!" Bill said, and put his finger over his lips and winked as if he was telling me that he could keep a secret. "The things you do see! All in one day. I'm'a go home and tell Gladys I saw a coon and a bear and an Indian all on the side of the road. Amazing things a snowstorm does bring out. That is one amazing suit! Get me one of them, I'd stay warm in the deep freeze! How'd he get it on? It seems to sort of fit real snug all around. I don't see no zipper or nothing. Say, Mister, you want a ride anywhere?"

My dad had shambled up through the snow and reached us.

"Dad," I said, "this man says there's an Indian museum nearby."

"Shore is," Bill said. "About thirty, thirty-five miles up the road." Bill looked my father up and down. "That shore is some suit. You want a ride? I can give you a ride. Take me a while cause the plowing goes slow, but you'll get there quicker than if you went on foot. If those are feet. What are those? Darn if it don't look like you have hands down there instead of feet. What'd you say your name was? You just pack up your tent there and sling it in the back, and we can all three squeeze in the truck easy. I don't mind. You go ahead."

So Dad and I went back to our tent and took it down and packed it up, although mostly Dad did it. The snow was so deep that he couldn't drag the wagon to the road. He picked it up and carried it over his head, hopping through the snow, and put the wagon down in the open back of the pickup truck. We had so much stuff that the truck settled down very deep on its springs. Dad tied the wagon down so that it wouldn't roll around on the truck bed. Then we climbed in the front seat with Bill, me in the middle because I was the smallest, and Dad next to the window, all squished up, his head bent down and his stomach bulging out over the dashboard.

"I never," Bill said, starting up the engine and moving slowly along the road, plowing as he went. "You must be one strong Indian. I never did see anyone that could lift up a thing like that and sling it around so easy. You aught to be more careful so you don't rip your suit. That is some suit. I wish I had me one of those suits. I only got one suit and the cat's been all over it so much it looks like about as hairy as yours. Ha ha! Well, I'm always trying to get that cat outside, but Gladys, that's my wife, she's always putting it back in the house. I puts her out, Gladys puts her in, till the cat she don't show up no more and I figure she's outside finally getting some healthy air and chasing a bird or something, and you know what? That darn cat's got into my closet and is sleeping on my clothes! That's where she's got to. That is the laziest cat I ever did see. Well, unless it's my cousin Danny's cat. Let me tell you about that cat. One day we were. . . ."

Dad and I sat quietly and let him talk on and on. He never took a break, and he never seemed to mind that we didn't contribute anything to the conversation. After a while I didn't even hear what he was saying. We got to Stockton after sundown, too late to visit the Indian museum. Bill pulled to the side of the road and Dad squeezed himself out of the front seat. He had been scrunched up inside for so long, about an hour and a half, that he could hardly stand up straight, and he was only about six and a half feet tall. He was so stiff that I had to help him untie our wagon. Then he was limbered up enough to lift it out of the truck and put it on the roadside. We said goodbye to Bill and thanked him for the ride, and he wished us luck and drove away.

"See, Jem," my dad said. "There's a nice man, even if he does talk a lot. He didn't mind that I'm an orangutan."

"Maybe he didn't realize you were one," I said.

"How could he not *realize*?" Dad said. "Jem, your brain has frozen up in the cold."

Dad dragged our wagon just out of town, which wasn't very far, because the town was only one or two streets. Then we set up our tent hidden in some trees and crawled inside to wait for the morning.

YE OLDE
INDIAN MUS-
EUM

8

The museum didn't open until eleven in the morning. Dad stayed home in our tent working on the ship's log. I thought I had deciphered everything useful in it, but he was systematic and wanted to write out a complete document in English. I decided to spend the morning looking around the town. I had lived my whole life in the city and had never seen anything like Stockton New York.

The whole town was only one crossroads. One of the roads, the one we had come along, had only two lanes with hardly anybody driving on it. The other one was a gravel road with no street sign. One corner had a gas station and a store that went with the station. The store was called "UPERMARKET" because the S had fallen off a while ago. Another corner of the crossroads had a diner with a striped canvass awning hanging over the front door. The awning was mostly covered with snow and the diner was closed. I saw a dog walking through the town and sniffing everywhere. It looked at me suspiciously. I'm sure it knew I was a stranger. It probably knew every person in the town. It must have decided I was okay, because it wagged its tail at me and went on with its busy schedule of sniffing.

All together about twenty houses marched back from the crossroads. They were miscellaneous, some of them very big with old-fashioned porches and wooden columns at the corners of the porch, and some of them more like shacks that had been put up with scrap wood. They all looked a little paint-peeled, but maybe the snow did that to them after a few years. A good half of the houses had Christmas lights out, and plastic reindeer and plastic Santas in their front yards, and I thought it must look fantastic in the dark when all the lights were turned on. I was sorry we hadn't had time to look at it properly the night before.

The snow was already melting, and the air was warm and the sun was hot, and I had to un-zipper my arctic coat and leave it open at the front or I would have sweated to death. I tucked my hat and mittens in my pockets and tried to avoid the mud puddles where the snow was turning to slush. Now and then I would hear a rushing sound like an avalanche and see a great big sheet of snow slide off of somebody's roof. One time such a large amount fell off, and made such a racket on a row of tin garbage cans lined up beside the house, that the town dog leaped in the air about three feet and ran off up the gravel road, looking back over his shoulder as if he thought it was my fault.

A lot of people were outside shoveling off their front steps or shoveling out around their cars, which had gotten blocked in quite a bit from the snow-plows. It must have been a pleasure to shovel snow on a sunny day like that, with the warm air taking care of most of your work for you. A lot of people said hi to me, or waved, or smiled as I went past, and I said hi back to them, although I was surprised and had never heard of anything like it before. In the city, nobody says hello to you unless they know you. Strangers never say anything except, maybe, "Hey Kid, get out of there," if they think you're snooping around with no good reason. So there was some advantage to a small town.

I went to the Upermarket and bought a breakfast bagel, the kind with buttery scrambled eggs and a nice greasy disk of sausage. I took it outside and sat on one of the cement blocks at the head of a parking space.

While I was sitting and eating, I had a long think,

and decided that our way of camping out was just about right. It couldn't be improved. We had plenty of tasty food; plenty of warmth in the tent, because it turns out that an orangutan is a furnace and generates a lot of heat; plenty of towns and people to meet. It was better than being a mountain climber. My dad had been telling me about the people who climb Mount Everest, and I was glad to be here in Stockton New York eating a delicious breakfast bagel instead of up on top of that mountain. Apparently they eat dried beans that have been soaked in snow water and heated up, if they can eat anything at all, especially since their fingers keep falling off and so I imagine it is hard to hold a spoon. They don't have a lot of warmth to go around among them. And as to meeting people, my dad said that you meet a lot of people along the way up there, but they're not very talkative, being dead and frozen up like mummies all along the main path. I think maybe they were so sick of eating dried beans in snow water that they just stopped eating all together and keeled over of starvation.

When I was done with my bagel I walked to the Indian museum, even though it wasn't open for another half hour, just to see what it looked like on the outside. It was right near the crossroads. It was an old wooden house, with gabled windows on the second floor and curly wooden carvings under the eves and no paint on it anywhere. It must have been one of the first houses built here, it had such an old fashioned look to it, and was so different from all the modern ones put up around it. It had a sign outside that said, "Amazing Indian History Museum!" I shaded the front window with my hands and peered inside, but it was so dim I couldn't see much except a lot of shelves.

"Hey Kid!" someone shouted, and I turned around and looked everywhere, but I couldn't see who was talking.

"Up here," the voice said. I looked up and saw a man standing on the roof of the next house over. It wasn't really a house; it was a trailer set up on cinderblocks. The man was using a broom to clean the snow off of his satellite dish. "Hey Kid," he said, looking over the edge of the roof at me, "you want to see the museum?"

"Sure," I said. "But it's not open yet."

"That's okay," he said. He tilted up his head, opened his mouth, and bellowed, "Hey Shirley! Some kid wants to see the museum!"

An upper window on the museum house banged opened and a voice said, "He got money? It's five dollars."

"Hey Kid," the roof guy said, "you got money? It's five dollars."

"Um, yeah," I said, feeling in my pocket just to make sure.

I waited for Shirley to come downstairs and open the front door. I didn't think Shirley sounded like an Indian name. When she unlocked the door and opened it for me, I didn't think she looked very Indian at all. She looked more like an English grammar teacher. She was thin and had short iron-gray hair and glasses. She turned on the light in the museum and looked at me severely, as if I had done something wrong. "Well?" she said.

I handed her a five-dollar bill, and she took it and put it in her cash register. "You have half an hour," she said. "Don't make me wait any longer. Don't touch anything if it has a sign on it that says don't touch. And don't take anything. I can smell a thief. I have a special nose."

"Yes, Ma'am," I said.

"And don't be smart," she added.

I wasn't trying to be smart; just polite. But I let it go, because there was no point in arguing. I turned and started to look through the museum. It seemed to fill up the four or five rooms of the downstairs part of the house. The first room didn't look promising. It was mainly full of brick-brack stuck with price tags, jewelry and shiny rocks and bits of carved wood that didn't have much to do with Native Americans. Also

Shirley was standing behind the counter glaring at me, and she made me nervous. I sidled out to the next room. I had only got there when the bell on the door tinkled and I heard Shirley yelp, "Goodness! What is it!"

I had a pretty good idea what it was. I looked back into the first room and saw my dad stepping into the museum.

"Hello," he said cheerfully, bounding across the room to the counter. "I'd like to look around."

"You'd what?" she said faintly, hanging onto the counter.

"Look through the exhibits. I think I just saw my son come in. Yes, there he is." He waved at me, and I waved back.

She looked him up and down and tried to speak a few times. Then she took a breath to steady herself and said, her voice a little more shrill than before, "It's ten dollars for an adult. But it'll be twenty for you. You're about the size of two adults. I don't suppose a thing like you has any money?"

Of course he did, and he put a twenty-dollar bill onto the counter. She picked it up and looked it over suspiciously. "All right," she said. "You have half an hour. Don't touch anything if it has a sign on it that says don't touch."

By that time five or six faces were peering into

the front window of the house, looking at Dad. I recognized the man next door who had come down from his roof. He was still holding his broom. There were other people too; we seemed to have brought out most of the town. Shirley strode over to the door and snarled, "What do *you* all want? You plan on paying the fee, or are you just going to block my door?"

"Shirley," one man said, "what *is* that?"

"Don't point at my customers!" she snapped. "If the Sasquach wants to come down out of a snow storm and look at my collection, he's welcome to, so long as he pays. If none of you want to pay the ten dollars to get in, you better clear off."

Of course, none of them wanted to pay, so they left the window.

"Now," Shirley said to us, "I'll give you thirty-one minutes, as a bonus, because those people were rude to you and I don't tolerate any rudeness. You better get cracking, though, because in thirty-one minutes you'll have to pay up a second time."

Dad and I thanked her politely. When we stepped into the next room, Dad slid up to me and said in a low voice, "Man, what a bat! Look at the crazy junk she's put together. I hope there's something useful buried in here."

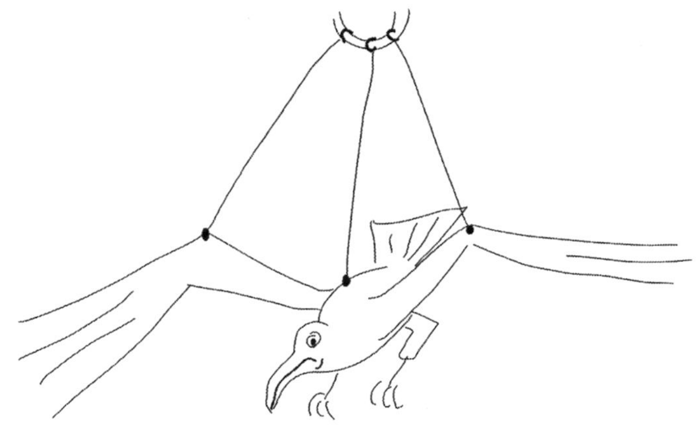

The stuffed eagle looked like it would rather be someplace else.

9

The first thing I saw was a skull. A human skull, yellowed and covered in dust and with a card taped to its forehead that said, “Do not touch!” I couldn’t help it. I looked around to make sure nobody was watching, and I tapped on it with my fingernail. It made a plastic sound. When I looked closely, I could see the seams where the plastic pieces had been stuck together in the factory. It looked so real that it gave me the creeps anyway.

Next to the skull was a stuffed eagle hanging from the ceiling on wires, its wings spread out about five feet across. It was wider than I was tall. I knew it was real, because it was moldy and frayed and falling apart, and had bald patches on its wings and back, in addition to the natural bald patch on its head. Its mouth was turned down at the corners and its glassy eyes stared at me as if it were saying,

"Ugh! Get me out of here!" But I couldn't do anything for it.

Next I came across an old fashioned, square piano that was broken and had about half its keys left. I could see that a skull might be related to Indians, since they presumably had skulls the same as any other people, and I could see how an eagle might have lived in the same general area as the Indians, but I didn't understand how the piano fit into the equation. A tag on the instrument said, "Pianos were sometimes used by settlers who lived near the Indians." That seemed like a stretch to me. It seemed like the museum was a collection of broken junk that had somehow accumulated over the years and was nine-tenths fraud.

The whole house was dim, because so many shelves and cabinets blocked the windows and the unblocked parts of the windows were covered in dust. A glass case loomed out of the shadows, and I saw a stuffed lamb in it. I stared at the lamb for a few seconds, wondering what it had done, but I couldn't see anything remarkable about it. Next to the lamb, a bookshelf contained neat rows of stones that had been picked up around the area. Some of them were round and polished and sparkling with minerals, and some of them were regular gray blobs, and all of them were dusty. Next to the rocks, hung up on the wall, was a tomahawk. It was a hatchet with a stone axe head and a carved wooden handle and feathers hanging from the end of the handle. It was so old and gray and so delicately carved that for the first time I was convinced I was seeing a real Indian artifact. I stared at that tomahawk for a while and wondered if it had been used to kill anybody. It made the shivers go down my spine.

Next to the tomahawk, a rake and a shovel leaned against the wall, along with a dried up wooden fence post with some twists of rusty barbed wire stapled to it. I suppose the farm implements represented the settlers again; but the shovel looked like it might have been bought at Sears.

As I was studying a table with old Dutch coins displayed under the glass top, my dad called me to the other side of the room. I had to walk carefully around the tables and chairs and claptrap everywhere. I almost tripped over a wooden crate of old fashioned soda bottles. My dad was staring at a map that was framed and hung on the wall. I could hardly see it in the dimness.

"Look," he said eagerly, pointing with his gigantic finger. "It's just what we need. A map of the tribal territories. Leo made land around Connecticut or Rhode Island and that would have put him right in with the Mahican tribe. That's the big yellow patch here, you see. They'd have taken him inland to their capital village, next to the Hudson River. Only it wasn't called that of course. It's labeled 'Mahicanituck.' Much nicer name for a river!"

I touched the map gently with my finger. "Look Dad, their capital city's called. . . ." I had to pause and think about it; "Pempotowwuthut-Muhhecannewuw. Wow. *That's* a name."

"He must have gone there," my dad said. "That's the most likely place. It's right around Albany, so we're going in exactly the correct direction. Right up the Hudson Valley. Let's take a look at those books."

About a dozen giant old hard covers were stacked on top of each other in a dark corner of the room. My dad was too big to fit into the corner, so I had to crouch down and scan the titles. One of them was, "The Gambler" by Fyodor Dostoyevsky. I didn't think that had anything to do with Indians. About halfway down I found a book called "Tribes of the North East," which looked promising. My dad stood guard in case Shirley came snooping around, and I pulled the book out of the stack. We took it to a window and leafed through it.

"Listen to this, Jem," Dad said, half reading and half paraphrasing. "The Mahicans were a democratic nation of about forty villages. The leader or sachem lived in Albany, New York. I mean, in Pempotowwuthut-Muhhecannewuw. Then, in 1609, Jem, think about it, only about 90 years after Leonardo, Henry Hudson came swaggering in with a band of Dutch settlers. Then it's the same old story. It's horrible. Fighting, disease, relocation, and the Mahicans were mostly gone from the area. Well. It'll be hard to find any lore from before Henry Hudson, since he mostly stamped it out."

"Keep reading Dad," I said. "Maybe something will turn up."

"Here's the Legend of the Geshoch. The sun, it says. No, that's not it."

"What about," I said, pointing to the next page, "the Legend of the Mahkwa. That looks like a bear."

"Right," he said. "But it doesn't seem informative for us."

"Then what about the Legend of the Cave?" I said. The book had only one short paragraph on the legend of the cave. As Dad began to read it to himself I could hear his breath sucking in sharply. I read it over his arm, and this is what it said:

"According to legend, long before the Dutch came, an old white man built a pair of wings that allowed him to fly. Every day he flew up to a cave high on a cliff in the Catskill Mountains. Nobody else could reach the cave, and in solitude he communed with his magic. The cave was considered to be a holy place and is said to be near Ipskunk, New

York, South of Albany and twenty miles west of the Grand Skid Cinema Complex, a must-see for cinema lovers."

I could see the book trembling in Dad's hands. "Jem," he said, in a hoarse whisper.

"I see it Dad," I whispered back. I was just as excited as he was. "That's it. Now we know where to go."

A voice barked out from behind us and startled us so much that we jumped and turned around. When my dad landed again on the floor, the whole room shook, and the shelves rattled, and items clattered on the floor all around us. The eagle swung on its wires and looked like it was trying to fly away.

"Time's up!" Shirley said. "And you're touching the exhibit! That book's an exhibit! Didn't I tell you not to touch anything?"

"It doesn't have a sign on it," I said, "so we thought it was okay."

She slapped her hand on the book with a bang, and when her hand came away, underneath was a post-it note that said, "Do not touch!" She glared at us and said, "It's got a sign now, and you're still touching it."

I held it out to her, and she snatched it away.

"I didn't know Sasquach could read," she said, peering at Dad through her glasses.

"Not only can I read," Dad said, "but I'd like to buy that book."

She stared at him, and then glared at the book in her hands. "That'll be thirty dollars," she said. "That's a fine old book. You have thirty dollars?"

Dad had a wad of cash tucked into his boot, and he took it out and paid for the book. As we were leaving the museum, Shirley snarled at us, "You have a good day." Then she grumbled, "I suppose a Sasquach has to go to school and learn to read, same as anybody. I wonder what he does for a living, though. Rescues snowmobilers, maybe. Seems to make a good income." I don't think she was really a mean person inside. I think it was just the way her voice came out. A lot of people in New York City are that way too.

Noma.

10

When we left the town that afternoon, a crowd of about thirty people came out to watch. They talked to each other but they didn't say anything directly to us. One of them took pictures, and I suspect the pictures ended up framed in the Amazing Indian History Museum. Even the dog came back and wagged its tail and seemed happy about the town party, and ate a sandwich out of somebody's hand, when the person was looking at us instead of at his sandwich. I sat on top of our wagon, way up where I could look around and see the entire town. Dad pulled us through the slush onto the main road, and then we continued on our way.

We didn't make very good speed. Dad said it was hard to pull through the slush. Later in the day the temperature began to drop, the slush turned to ice, and the wagon moved even slower and jerked around quite a bit. I didn't sit on top anymore. I didn't want to add to Dad's load, and also I didn't want to pitch off in a skid. Sometimes a car would go past, driving slowly because of the bad road conditions. It would come up behind us, slow down and open a window, and we would see a person's head sticking out to ask if we needed help. Then the person would spot Dad. If the person was wearing a hat, the hat would fly off the top of his head. If the person was drinking coffee from a paper cup, the cup would fly out of the window and the coffee would spill all over the snow. If the person had eyeballs, which most of them did, the eyeballs would shoot out about sixteen inches and then rebound back into the person's head with the optic nerves twisted around. Then the window would roll shut and the car would shoot past, dangerously above the speed limit. I was afraid we'd cause an accident on that icy road and hurt somebody. But mostly I wished that one of those drivers would be nice enough to stop and help us. I was no good pulling the wagon, and I thought my dad could use a break. We were about fifty miles from Ipskunk and the road was beginning to slant uphill.

"Dad," I said after a while, "I have an idea. Let's write out a sign, and I can flash it at the cars as they go by. Then somebody might stop and help."

"Oh brilliant," Dad said. He was becoming grumpy from the exercise. "Absolutely. We're obviously not noticeable enough as it is."

"I thought I could write, 'Indian Shaman in Bear Costume, Needs Ride.' Then people wouldn't be as scared off."

"What!" my dad said. "Jem! That's a lie!"

"It's almost true," I said. "But if you want to pull that thing for another fifty miles, we can forget the sign."

He groaned and said, "Oh, go ahead then."

I took some blank paper and a pen and drew our sign in big block letters. Then we parked the wagon on the roadside and both sat on top of it, side by side, me holding up the sign, Dad leafing through the Tribes book. For a long time nobody drove by. The road was probably never frequently used, and now it was sheeted in ice. The people who lived along it were most likely at home already. The wind blew my dad's hair around. I didn't mind if the wind went from me to him. But sometimes it switched around and blew his long wispy orange hair into my face and right up my nose.

"Achoo!" I said. "Dad. When we find that cave, can we live in it? I always wanted to be a cave man."

Dad looked up from the book, his fingernail pressed down where he had left off reading. "Hm?" he said. "Oh, it'll be a while before we find it, I expect. Might be in the spring. Or next year. Who knows. There's probably hundreds of caves we'll have to explore. But we'll find it in the end."

"I wonder," I said, "if he carved his initials on the wall? You know, 'LDV wuz here'. Otherwise it'll be hard to know if we found the right place."

"That's a good point," Dad said. "What exactly did he leave behind? I'm hoping we'll find the remains of his ornithopter. That was the flying machine he invented. It had leather wings that flapped like a bird's, and you worked it by pulling on metal handles. The plans are in his notebooks."

"Maybe we'll find his skeleton," I said. "That would be creepy. I don't know if I'd live in a cave that had a skeleton in it."

"It wouldn't hurt you," Dad said. "Skeletons mainly mind their own business. But Jem, quick, get your sign ready, someone's coming."

We watched an old rusty station wagon crawling up the road. When it came near us I held out our sign and waved it around. I thought the car would accelerate as soon as the driver saw Dad, but it didn't. It stopped next to us and an old lady rolled down the window and looked out. She had to crane her head up to see us, because we were sitting ten feet above the road. At first I thought she might be so old and blind that she hadn't properly seen Dad.

Then I thought that if she was so blind, we might not want her to drive us.

"Hello Indians," she said cheerfully. She couldn't have been too blind to read my sign. "My, you look cold out there." Her face was creased and swirled like a pool of mud that had gotten stirred around with a stick. Under the wrinkles I could see she had wide cheekbones and a high forehead, and her hair, which had gone gray but was still streaked with black, was pulled back behind her head. Her eyes sparkled at us, and all at once I had the thought that she was an Indian, a real one, a Native American, and not fake like we were. She was a tiny woman who could barely see over the steering wheel. She looked about ninety years old. "I don't think you can fit your wagon in my car," she said in her cheerful but brittle old-lady's voice. "You can tie it behind, if you like. I think," she added, looking Dad up and down, "that the boy had better sit in the front seat next to me, and the man in the bear suit had better lie down in back. I don't suppose you'll fit otherwise. I do like a big man with a hairy chest."

Dad winked at me and grinned. He tied our wagon handle to the back bumper with rope, and then crawled into the back seat of the station wagon. He could just fit, his head up against one door and his big feet up against the opposite door. I sat in the front seat and the little old lady drove down the road, very slowly because of the ice everywhere and the wagon in tow.

"What tribe are you from?" she asked politely, looking at my dad in the rear view mirror.

"Well, . . ." Dad said. His voice was muffled because his face was pressed into the door and the padded handle had gone partly into his mouth. "It's this way. See, we're . . . what I mean is . . . you could say we're Mahicans."

"Oh wonderful!" she said, smiling, her eyes sparkling, and I had the uncomfortable feeling that she knew perfectly well we were not. "You have a wonderful bear suit. It fits you very well. I'm not familiar with the bear species. When I first saw you, I thought you might be a Sumatran orangutan. But I'm sure that you know best."

"Good God," Dad said. "Jem! Did you hear that? The lady knows what she's talking about."

"Sometimes she does," the lady said, with a light, tinkling laugh. "Sometimes she doesn't. What is your Mahican name?"

"Uh," Dad said. "Carl. Carl Martin. And my son is Jem."

"Carl Martin," she repeated in her precise, old lady's voice. "Jem Martin. Very glad to meet you. Most people call me Noma. It's short for Nomasis, which means 'little grandmother' in Mahican." She laughed again. "I decided you were probably not a Native America shaman when I saw that you were studying the subject in a book. It seemed most unlikely."

"Well, okay," I said, jumping in because my dad had trouble talking around the upholstery. "It's a little embarrassing, but see, we couldn't think of any other way to get people to stop for us. Everyone gets scared of my dad and drives away. We thought that if he was an Indian shaman, maybe they'd be less scared, or more curious. And we really wanted to get a ride to Ipskunk."

"Quite understandable," she said, smiling at me. "And it certainly worked. I *am* curious. Do you live in Ipskunk?"

"Oh no," I said. "We're looking for Leonardo da Vinci."

"Of course," she said, politely. "I should have guessed. Under what circumstances did you hope to meet him?"

"In a cave," I said. "Not him exactly. Well, maybe his skeleton."

"Jem!" Dad sputtered around the door handle. "You're getting at it from the wrong direction. Tell her from the beginning, and maybe she can help. She might know." So I told her the whole story, starting with my dad turning himself into an orangutan and us getting kicked out of our home. She shook her head at that part. I told her about our quest, and how we had traced Leonardo across the Atlantic to North America, and realized that he must have taken up with the local Indians. Then I told her about the legend of the cave, and her eyes glittered and she had an odd smile on her face as she drove.

When I was done, she said, "What a beautiful story. I'm so glad I stopped to give you a ride. And now you want to know if I can help you? I certainly know about the legend of the cave."

"You do?!" Dad sputtered. "Do you know the right cave?"

"I might," she said. "But that's hard to prove. There's more than one cave that might fit the legend. Six or seven, I believe. But the one that I'm thinking of is special. It's the only one that nobody has been able to reach. Ever since I was a little girl I wanted to explore it, but it's quite inaccessible. When I was fifteen I broke my leg trying to climb the cliff face, and when I was thirty I broke my wrist. I'm afraid I rather stopped trying after that. I've seen a few rock climbers shake their heads and give up because the cliff is too full of rubble."

"I bet that's the one!" Dad said. "I bet that's Leonardo's cave!"

"I don't know about that," she said. "The legend of the cave always seemed, well, *legendary* to me. Merely an excuse to explore a new cave. I'd hazard a guess that my special cave is filled up mostly with old bird's nests."

"Bah!" my dad said. "It has an ornithopter in it."

"All the same," she said, "I wish . . . I still do wish I could see the inside of it. I admit, however, I'm a little old for spelunking. Do you know, when I was little, I used to look up at that cliff and think, if only I were a monkey, I'm sure I could climb it. If I had four hands I could climb anything. Carl Martin, I will make a deal with you. I'll show you where my cave is. In return, if you can reach it, throw me down a rope. I'll tie it around my waist and you can pull me up."

"It's a deal!" my dad roared, sticking his hand forward between the two front seats. Noma's hand was so small and fragile that she could only manage to grasp one of Dad's fingers, but she shook the finger, and the deal was made.

We drove four hours along that icy road at a creeping rate, up into the Catskills through a tangle of back roads, onto a gravel lane that seemed more like a rutted driveway, and reached Ipskunk late in the evening. The sun had long gone down, and there was no point trying to climb anything until the next morning. Noma drove us to her house. I got out and pulled on my dad's arm to help him slide out of the back seat. He had to lie on the ground in the snow for a few minutes to expand to his proper size, and then he could stand up all right.

Noma's house was a little one-story cottage that she said her father had built. It was on a saddle in the mountains, several miles from any town. It was made out of old gray weathered boards, and had a front porch about big enough for a single chair, and one window, and a metal pipe sticking out of the roof that must have been the chimney. My dad could never have fit through the door. She said we could set up our tent in her yard, if we wanted to, and stay for the night. Or, if we liked, we could sleep in the barn.

Her house was in a clearing in the trees, lit up by the moonlight so that the slate roof seemed to glow. Away from the house, just under the branches of the woods, stood a spooky dark barn. The front window was covered over in wire and looked like a snarling mouth with braces. She said the barn used to have goats in it, but hadn't been used except by barn swallows for about thirty years, and was probably good protection against the wind. Dad would have slept in it, but I didn't want to. I wanted our warm, comfortable tent.

Dad unhitched our wagon from the car and put up the tent in the moonlight beside Noma's house. Noma watched him, standing in the snow and clutching her shawl around herself to keep warm. She must have been amazed at how good he was with his hands and feet. He set up the tent in record time. I bet it was less than two minutes.

"If you can't climb up to that cave," she said, "I don't think anyone can."

"How far away is it?" Dad said. "Can we get there early in the morning?"

"As early as you wish," she said, smiling at him and pointing. "It's right there. Didn't you realize?"

About hundred yards from the house, a giant rubbley cliff rose up out of the trees and slanted up in the moonlight. It was just far enough from the house that if a boulder fell off the cliff it probably wouldn't smash through the roof.

"Now you know why it's my special cave," she said. "I've been looking at it all my life. Good night, Carl Martin. Good night, Jem Martin!" She turned around, hobbled to her little house, and went inside.

Dad and I crawled into our tent. I wanted to go to sleep, but Dad lit some candles, sat down and clutched his head between his hands. "Jem! How can we sleep? That might be the cave up there! I think I saw it. A kind of a dark spot. What if we find something that belonged to him? My god! I don't know if I can wait. Maybe I should try it now, in the moonlight."

"Dad, don't be ridiculous!" I said. "It's just starting to snow. Anyway, do you know what night it is?"

"No. What?"

"It's Christmas eve. I think. Tomorrow is Christmas day."

"You're right! I totally forgot about it! Good thinking, Jem. Merry Christmas. I suppose I should be good and wait till morning to unwrap the present."

He blew out the candles and curled up in his blanket. During the night I woke up a few times, and in the faint glow of moonlight through the tent roof I could see his massive furry back rising and falling with his breathing. But he wasn't snoring. He was probably lying awake thinking about that cave.

Cliff
Cave
Dad
Noma
Me

11

"Good morning, Indians!" Noma said, knocking on the metal surface of the wagon that made up a wall of our tent. "I thought you wanted to get up early?"

My dad and I woke up together. We had had an exhausting few days, and had overslept. Dad must have dropped off finally in the early morning. He sat up bleary and stared at his watch through the tangles of hair over his eyes. "Jem!" he groaned. "It's ten thirty."

We crawled outside. Noma had made hot pancakes for us, and I sat on her front steps and ate them with maple syrup. They were delicious, but Dad couldn't digest them, so he ate three cabbages.

After breakfast, we walked to the barn. Noma thought that some of the old farm equipment might be useful for climbing a cliff. I didn't see how anything in a goat barn would help us. But it turned out that the barn had been used as a garbage dump and a storage shed, and was piled up to the ceiling in places. It was a good thing we hadn't tried to sleep in it the night before, because we would have walked into about six rusty circular saw blades, and a roll of wire fencing, and a broken tractor engine, and an old fashion car that had been taken apart so it could fit in through the front door, and shovels and picks and saws and screwdrivers and wooden boxes of roofing nails, and lots of old furniture, and a stack of newspapers from about fifty years ago, and the dried up skeleton of a ground squirrel that had crawled in there in the distant past, and I don't know what else was buried in that pile.

"Oh dear," Noma said standing in the doorway, the sun shafting in behind her and lighting up the jumble on the concrete floor, "I had forgotten how full it was."

Dad rummaged around, climbing over the teetering piles of junk into a back room, and after some banging and crashing sounds, he came back out with a big wooden spool of rope. When the rope from the barn was tied onto the rope from our wagon, we had about four hundred feet of it, and that seemed like enough.

We walked along a path through the snowy woods until we reached the cliff. The bottom part of the cliff rose up jumbled and broken out of the for(The slant was shallow enough that we could climb up quite a long distance. Noma seemed to have an easy trail worked out; she stepped from one rock to the next without a lot of strain. Then the serious part of the cliff rose up out of the rubble, and that's where we had to stop.

Probably that cliff had been straight up and down once, a thousand years ago, but a giant wedge of the front surface had fallen off. That must have been where all the rubble came from. The cliff face was slanted the wrong way. It didn't slant back away from us; it slanted out over our heads. If you climbed it, you would be hanging out over empty space most of the time. Maybe if you had sticky pads on your feet and hands you could climb it, but even then I wouldn't have wanted to try, because the rock all along the cliff looked brittle and full of shards that might break off as you grabbed them.

"There it is," Noma said cheerfully, pointing up. "There's the cave." About three hundred feet up the cliff the sunlight poured into a gaping hole. From underneath we could see a bit of the roof of the cave, but that was all. It looked like a good-sized opening.

"Right," Dad said, looking up and around and inspecting the cliff closely. I couldn't see how he would succeed, but he didn't look discouraged. He scratched at his head and then limbered up his fingers and toes, and then wound the rope around his waist so that he could lower it down to us once he got to the cave. I mean, *if* he got to the cave. For the first time, I began to worry about him.

"Right," he said again. "This should be easy. Should take a minute. Three minutes, tops. I tell you. Look at it. I can go from here to that spot with the crack there, and then to that other spot with the twisty plant growing out of it, and then to. . . . Well, I'll figure it out once I get to that spot. Here goes."

He crouched on all fours and then, as if he had springs coiled up in his arms and legs, Boing, he leaped into the air about fifteen feet. I had never seen him do that before. It was incredible. He was so heavy that I didn't think he could leap very high. But he didn't look heavy now. He looked as light and agile as a spider. He turned over in mid air and landed splayed out against the rock face, clutching on by his hands and feet. Then he paused for a moment, looking around for the next hold.

"Dad!" I said. "That's amazing! How did—"

"Jem," he said, "don't talk. I need to think."

I closed my mouth. Noma and I sat on some comfortable smooth rocks that were lying nearby. I think maybe Noma had put them there a long time ago as seats. It was a nice place to sit in the morning, the sunlight on our faces, the rocks and the snow sparkling around us, but I couldn't enjoy it while Dad was clinging above us and might fall any second.

He seemed frozen to the spot, only his head moving, swiveling around like a giant bug searching for prey. Then one hand let go and moved two inches to a new spot. That was all. Then he was still again for about five minutes. I thought he had given up and was about to jump back down. I thought he had finally realized how impossible the cliff was. But suddenly his arms and legs went into motion, and he zipped up the cliff about another ten feet. He seemed to know exactly where to put his hands and feet. I suppose he had worked out the whole sequence in his head. Then he stopped again for another three or four minutes.

I could see that having four hands was useful, but I could also see that he was climbing mostly with his brain. After every little bit that he climbed, he would pause and think very carefully for minutes. Sometimes, after a pause he would climb back down to a previous point, and try again in a different direction. Sometimes it seemed like he was climbing sideways more that up. A few times, after five or ten minutes all he did was move one hand. At other times he might go fifteen or twenty feet all in one spurt. It was horrible and shivery to watch, but fascinating too. I never once saw him lose a hold on anything. He seemed to choose carefully, and nothing broke under his hands. Every now and then I saw him hang on with three limbs and pick the loose bits of rock off the cliff with his free hand, just to make sure that they didn't get in his way. The rock pieces fell down and smashed on the ground.

After about an hour he came near to the cave mouth, but it was no good; he couldn't reach it from that angle. Even I could see from below that the cave had a lip that stuck out. He couldn't get over it on one side of the cave and would have to try the other side. So down he came, about one hundred feet, backing off of the cave entrance to try another approach. That one didn't work either. But the third time he did better. I could see he was about six feet below the cave near the easiest corner. But the last bit shelved out from the cliff so steeply, and so smoothly, I didn't see how he could climb over it. He stayed in that one place just below the cave, perfectly still, looking tiny and black against the gray stone, hundreds of feet up. That was his longest pause. He stayed there for about fifteen minutes. Then suddenly those springs in his arms and legs let off again, and he boinged off of the cliff face, jumping out and up, and I screamed. I couldn't help it. I said, "Ack!" because if he missed his hold, he would fall a long way onto a hard ground and smash like a tomato. But he got his fingers over the cave ledge, and in another half a second had pulled himself up and disappeared in the cave.

"He did it!" I sang out. "Look at that! He got up there!"

Noma was smiling so hard she couldn't talk. Her eyes had disappeared in the wrinkles on her face.

Then, way up the cliff, my dad's head stuck out from the cave entrance and looked down at us.

"Ahoy!" he said, his voice faint from the distance. "Hello! What a view! Wow! Jem, you look like a bug! And Noma, your house looks as small as a sugar frosted mouse house! Hey! Watch out! Stand by! Get ready! Rope coming down!"

Slowly, the dark snake of the rope dangled down and down, until the end came down right in front of our faces and touched the ground at our feet.

"Noma first!" Dad shouted down. "Jem, you make sure she gets tied on securely."

Noma knew all about ropes and knots, and she made a kind of rope swing that she could sit in while holding tight. She also tied a safety loop around her waist, in case she lost her grip on the way up. "Oh my!" she said, when she started to rise up into the air, and then she was too far up for me to hear her brittle voice. Because the cliff was slanted out over our heads, she rose straight without bumping into anything. She had a cloth bag in her hands full of supplies that she had brought along, and it dangled beneath her and swayed. Dad pulled very fast, and I saw her disappear over the lip of the cave.

Then the rope came back down again. "Your turn, Jem," Dad called down. "Be careful!"

I sat in Noma's swing, held tight to the rope, and felt my feet lift off from the ground. I tried not to look down. I spun around on the rope as I was jerked upward, and a bird flew past me and glared at me out of its little shiny black eye as if it was outraged at the sight of a person flying. Before I had time to relax or get used to the motion, I was up, and Dad had lifted me over the lip of the cave and into the entrance.

"I told you it'd be easy," Dad said.

The view really was amazing. I could see out over the woods and hills for miles. The morning sun poured down onto everything, and I saw a stream far away shining from reflected sunlight as if it was a light bulb filament. I could see Noma's house practically under us. If I had thrown a stone, I might have gotten it down her chimney. The gravel road snaked away from her house and disappeared here and there under the snowy trees, until it reached a paved road, and the paved road stretched on down the hillside like some black paint that had run down the slope.

Much farther away I saw a collection of roofs sticking up like mushrooms. It must have been Ipskunk, New York. Even farther away I saw a lake that was a dull white, and I wondered if it was frozen over. I saw a car driving around the lake, and the car was only as big as a flea.

The mouth of the cave was about forty feet wide, and had a flat place in the front like a landing pad that was cluttered with sticks and dried up leaves. Birds must have brought them up there. Noma's whole house could have fit nicely into that front entrance. Farther back, the cave narrowed and turned into shadows and darkness.

Noma was standing with her hand on the cave wall to steady herself, peering over the edge at the humongous landscape. The wind blew around a few strands of gray hair that had come loose from her ponytail. The look on her face was eager and focused and alive. She took five or six deep breaths and then turned to us and said, "Now I've done everything, and I've seen everything. Carl Martin, you have made me happy."

Dad grinned at her, his orangutan mouth wide open and all his giant pegs of teeth showing.

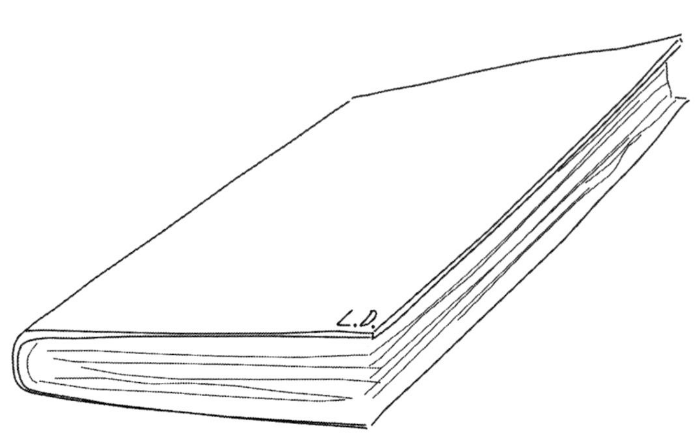
L.D.

12

"Let's explore," Dad said. "I can see there's enough room here to land an ornithopter. But he wouldn't have left it exposed. I'm sure it's in a back chamber of the cave somewhere. Jem, we should have brought candles. How silly of us!"

"Very silly," Noma said, smiling. "Luckily you brought someone less silly." She reached into her cloth bag of supplies, brought out three flashlights, and handed them around.

"Fantastic!" Dad said. "Thank you! You're brilliant! This is it. Jem, I can hardly breathe. Might be the altitude, but I think it's the excitement. I swear I thought it'd take us years, and here we've found the place already. Wow."

"Don't be too sure, Dad," I said. I didn't want him to get his hopes up too high. Now that we were in the cave, and I saw the rubble and sticks and dirt and leaves here and there, and the snow piled on the floor where the wind had left it, and no sign that anyone had ever been here before, I thought that Noma was probably right. It was just a regular cave. I looked around the walls, but I didn't see anything like initials, or any carving or cave painting. I wasn't very hopeful. But Dad was bounding up and down in excitement, his eyes wide open and his hair flying around.

"Come on!" he said. "Quick! Into the cave! Don't fall down any holes! Don't trip! Be careful! Hurry! Stay together! Don't get lost!" Shouting whatever came into his head, he bounded toward the shadows at the back of the cave.

The front entrance narrowed to a kind of passage that led into the cliff, slanting very slightly upward. I had never been in a cave before, and I was excited to explore it. But we had hardly gone anywhere, only about fifty feet, when the passageway ended. There was no more cave. No other caverns. The wall was solid, carved into funny twisty shapes by water. It glittered in the beams of our flashlights. There was no sign of a cave-in that might have blocked off an inner chamber. No, the cave simply ran out. We had found the end of it.

My dad stood dumbfounded. He had stopped bouncing and was perfectly still, looking at the back wall, his eyes stretched wide open and all the excitement gone from his face. I felt sorry for him. There wasn't any ornithopter. If anyone had ever been in this cave, there was no trace left. I shined the beam of my flashlight around the stone face, from side to side and top to bottom, looking for any carving. I thought that da Vinci, being an artist, might have carved a face or a foot or something. But no, there was nothing. Only a few small holes in the wall. I walked around peering into those holes, shining my flashlight into them, but they were nothing more than shallow pits. The largest one was about the size of an oven. It was a hollow spot where a big rock must have fallen out of the wall. There was still a fragment of rock lying inside it about the size of a bread loaf.

I reached into the hollow to pick up the rock fragment. When I touched it, it wasn't as cold or hard as I expected. It seemed spongy to me. I lifted it, and a load of gray dust fell off it and billowed up into the air, making me choke and cough. When I got my breath back, I said, "Dad, look, what is it? It's not a rock. It's too square."

Dad came back to life. He unfroze all of a sudden and hurried over to me. "Jem, be careful, don't drop it! Let's take it out where we can see it better."

I carried it out to the front porch of the cave. We

sat on the stone floor, all three of us, and I set the mysterious thing gingerly down between us.

"It might be a mummified snake," Noma said.

Dad poked it gently with his finger. I could see his finger trembling from excitement. "It was made by somebody," he said in a hushed voice. "It's a package wrapped up in leather. Look at the stitches." He brushed at it, cleaning off more grit and dust, revealing a row of thick brown stitches.

"You're right, Dad," I said. "It's our Christmas present. Go ahead, open it."

He lifted it carefully and turned it over in his hands a few times. "It's almost a shame to cut it open. I'm afraid I'll harm it. But with a little care. . . ." He picked at the stitches with his large yellow fingernails and tore them open one by one. Then he began to pull open the loosened edge. The leather wrapping was stiff and did not come off easily. I could see that it was incredibly old. Finally he unwrapped the object and held it out for us to see. It was a notebook. It was bound in black leather and had no title or name on the front.

Dad set it down on the floor and slowly, gently, lifted the front cover. It opened quite easily. It seemed to have been perfectly preserved inside of its wrapper.

The first page was a blank and yellowing sheet of

paper. The second page was crammed full of charcoal sketches and writing, and even I could see that it had been drawn by Leonardo. His style was unmistakable. I saw an eagle, and an otter, and some Indians, and some trees, and a canoe, and a hut made out of reeds, all drawn perfectly, sketched so that they looked even more real, somehow, than a photo would have done. You could imagine the actual things. Curled all around the drawings was his strange crabbed up handwriting.

Dad stared at the page for a long time. We all did. Then he said in a choked voice, "You found it Jem. You found it."

We spent most of the day up in that cave. Nobody wanted to leave. It was a beautiful place, and very comfortable, especially on the front porch in the sunlight. Noma had brought lunch for us, muffins and turkey sandwiches for me and her, and a large pile of carrots and asparagus for Dad. But Dad didn't eat very much. He was too excited. He didn't want the direct sunlight to harm the notebook, so he sat in the gloom about twenty feet into the cave to decipher it. If he had had his mirror and Italian-English dictionary, he would have made faster progress. But he did okay. Every now and then he'd read out to us something that he had just translated, while Noma and I sat in the sun and ate our lunches.

I tossed some muffin crumbs over the ledge for the birds. Some of those birds zipped past and snatched the crumbs right out of the air. Noma said they were swifts, and were the most acrobatic of birds. She sipped a special Indian tea out of a thermos. She let me taste it, but it was too bitter for me.

"Listen to this," Dad said. " 'If anyone should find my hiding place, know that I have gone immeasurably farther. Farewell.' "

"And listen to this," Dad said later. "'I have come to appreciate the wise and peaceful folk who live here. I will miss them. But I must move on.' Jem, he didn't stay in the area. This is amazing. It's fantastic. He went on another journey. We'll have to figure out where. Remember, we swore to find his final resting place. It's no good stopping the search here. Oh, this is fun! He left a clue for us!"

"Dad," I said, "maybe he was about to die."

"Jem! Don't be so morbid!" Dad said, shooting me a reproachful look.

Noma shook her head and took a sip of tea. "I think," she said quietly to me, "you're probably right. But your dad is very clever. I wouldn't discount his opinion. This morning I would never have guessed we'd find a treasure like that notebook. But there it is."

About an hour later, after Noma and I had finished our lunch and were sitting peacefully watching the world beneath us, Dad gave a long, low whistle. I hadn't known that he could, with an orangutan's lips. "My *God*!" he said. "Jem! Noma! Come and look. You and your morbid view of the thing, Jem. *This* is where he went. *This* is the somewhere else."

Noma and I came to look. Dad held open the book and we crouched beside him. The page was covered with technical diagrams of an invention, but I didn't know what it was meant to be. It looked like a wagon, or a car, full of gears and levers and other strange devices. Everything was labeled, but I couldn't read the handwriting.

"What does it say, Dad?" I asked.

"Ah, Jem, I should have expected it. Come to think of it, I *did* expect it. The man was a genius. It's a nuclear powered spaceship. Don't you see?"

"A *what*?" I said.

"Oh dear," Noma said. "That seems most unlikely."

"Of *course* it's unlikely," Dad said. "The whole *point* of an imagination is to do something unlikely. That's what Leonardo was all about: imagination. The next fifty pages are full of technical plans. He spells out exactly where he means to land on the moon. Don't you understand? He built a spaceship and went moonside. That's his final resting place. That's where his last notebook is." Dad put down the book and stared at me.

"Dad," I said, "are you saying—"

"Of course I am."

"But do you mean—"

"Yes."

"You want to—"

"Who wouldn't? We have the plans, don't we?"

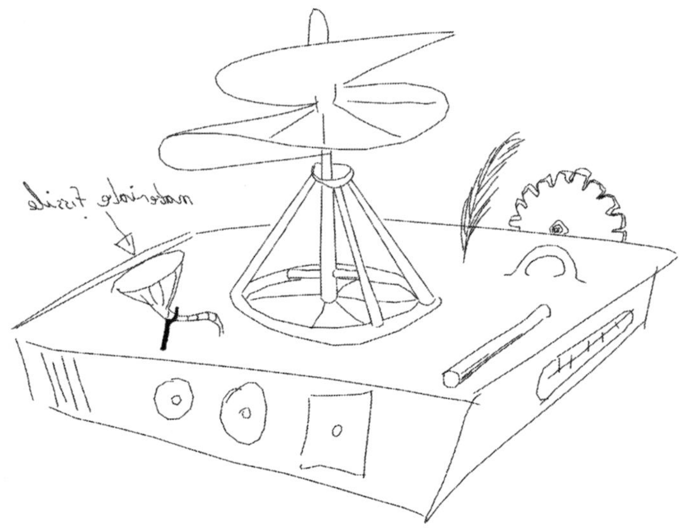

da Vinci's nuclear-powered spaceship drawing.

13

That is how we began our great ambitious adventure of building a spaceship and flying to the moon. Leonardo's plans were so neatly drawn and logically explained that Dad had no trouble understanding them. Our only difficulty was to find the necessary material.

The evening that we came down from the cave, Noma seemed quiet. At first I thought she must be feeling nostalgic and remembering all the times in her youth that she had tried to get into the cave. But it turned out that she was carefully thinking over an idea.

"Carl," she said at dinner. We ate together in our tent, because it was the only place that all three of us could get in the door. "And Jem. I've seen a lot of things today I never thought were possible. I've met a talking ape. I've seen the inside of my special cave, and I didn't think I would reach it in my lifetime. And I've seen a lost notebook of Leonardo da Vinci. My head is in a whirl right now and I'm beginning to think that anything is possible. I'm old, but I'd love to see the moon. And what have I got to lose? If you promise to take me with you, I'll let you use anything in my barn. Maybe some of the old equipment will help. If you take me with you," she added, "I might remember to bring lunch and a flashlight."

"Wow!" Dad said, a whole potato shooting out of his mouth and thudding into the wall of the tent. I had to duck or it would have given me a black eye. "Noma! Are you kidding? I could build six spaceships out of that material. That's all I need. I think I saw a small forge in the back room. I can use it to shape the metal. And I saw plenty of tools lying around. I better read up on those plans. Oh boy, this *will* be fun."

The next day my dad and I worked in the barn, organizing the junk into piles so that Dad could find whatever he was looking for. I spent the afternoon sanding the rust off of the tools while Dad sat in the shade of a tree and studied the notebook. Sanding tools is a sweaty job. It's not easy, and my arms were sore and my fingers turned orange, and my face was soon covered with rust stains from accidentally touching myself with my fingers. But I didn't mind.

I knew that my dad would end up doing most of the work, and I wanted to get in as much as I could while I had the chance. By the end of the day, I had a pile of shiny clean screwdrivers and pliers and saws and things like that.

For about three days, Dad did nothing more than read that notebook. He was thoughtful and quiet. He held the book every moment of the day. Sometimes he sat on a rock with his back against the side of the barn, sometimes he sat in our tent reading by candle light, and several times I saw him asleep at night with it gripped in his hands. He always put a sheet of plastic wrap over the open page so that he wouldn't speckle it with food that flew out of his mouth as he chewed. He didn't pay a lot of attention to his meals, and the only reason why he ate at all was because Noma and I kept piling a supply of cabbages and lettuces next to him. He would reach out absently, pick up a head of lettuce, and pop it in his mouth while his eyes never left the notebook. He mumbled to himself constantly, and if I asked him a question he might answer in some very peculiar way. Once I asked him if there was anything Noma and I could buy for him, since we were going to drive to the town. And he said, "Yes, Jem, I think you're right, it *is* a forward operating flank mechanism. Thank you."

Then, one day, Dad looked up from the notebook and said, "Jem! Where are you? Where'd you go?"

"Right here, Dad," I said. I came out of the barn where I had been neatening up, putting some old tires in a stack in the corner.

"It's time, Jem," he said. "I think I can build it. It's not hard at all. Quick! You pack our belongings, and tell Noma to pack hers, and I'll start building the spaceship. Let's see who's done first."

He didn't need to consult the notebook anymore; he had memorized every detail of it, and handed it to me to pack up with our belongings. Then he ran into the barn and seemed to turn into a flying windmill of arms and legs. I've already described how handy and, I suppose, footy, my dad could be in setting up our tent. It amazed me the first time I ever saw it. But that was nothing compared to now. He bounded from the front room of the barn to the middle room, where the goats had been kept, to the back room where the pails of goat milk used to be. It was filled up with neatly organized piles of farm implements, and he grabbed from this pile and snatched from that pile, and seemed to do six things at the same time. I saw him once unscrewing a part from an old tractor engine with his right hand, lifting a box of rivets with his left foot, sawing through a pipe with his left hand, and hopping around on his right foot, all at the same time, in a kind of a blur. His eyes seemed to pop out of his head, and he panted as if he was racing time. He set up a forge, which was a furnace where he could heat up metal and hammer it into different shapes. He melted together one of the blades from a circular saw, a pickaxe, a statue of George Washington, and the pendulum from a grandfather clock. I don't know what that particular part was for, but it sure looked strange.

He put our wagon in the middle of the barn. It seemed to make up the main body of the spaceship. Then he added to it. He welded on walls and struts and all kinds of gizmos. He used the arctic survival quilt and the explorer snow boots in the construction. He piled on engine parts and gears and loops of wire and the windows of an old car until the thing was an amazing jumble, all the metal parts melted crazily together, with a satellite dish stuck on top.

I spent the afternoon standing in the barn door watching my dad work, and now and then Noma came over and stood next to me so that she could watch too. It was a treat to see.

Around six o'clock, when the sun was down and the barn was so filled up with shadows that Dad couldn't work anymore, he took hold of the wagon handle and wheeled the contraption outside.

"There!" he said.

"You sure did a lot, Dad," I said. "How much longer before it's done?"

"It *is* done," he said. "Can't you see? Now you can put all our belongings inside, and we'll set off tonight."

"Um, . . ." I said. I hadn't packed anything.

"Carl," Noma said, "what does it run on?"

"Good gracious!" Dad shouted, leaping up in the air and slapping his hand onto his furry forehead. "I forgot the fuel! It needs nuclear fuel, of course. I didn't find any in the barn. Do you have any in the house?"

"I'm sorry," Noma said. "I don't keep any nuclear fuel."

"You don't?" Dad said, outraged. "Why not?! Old Spork used to keep a barrel of it in his kitchen under the sink. Now what are we going to do?"

"Um, Dad," I said, "how exactly did Leonardo get *his* nuclear fuel?"

"He mined it, of course. What do you think? When he saw glowing rocks, that's what gave him the idea of building a spaceship. Genius, I tell you. But it'll take us months to mine enough, even if we can find the right place to dig. And we'd need a permit."

"What about glow-in-the-dark clocks?" I said.

"I have one of those," Noma said. "You're of course welcome to use it."

"Glow in the dark . . . glow in the. . . ." Dad paused and thought for a moment. "If we get enough of them," he said, "and scrape off the radium into the fuel tank, it would work, of course. But we'd need a darn lot of them."

Since we couldn't think of any other solution, we decided that Noma and I would drive through the nearby towns and buy all the glow-in-the-dark clocks we could find. Dad would stay behind with the spaceship. Noma said that he aught to concentrate on fine-tuning the mechanism. But the real reason was to avoid a stir if he showed up in town. It was simpler to leave him behind. Besides, I don't think he enjoyed riding in a car. It was too cramped for him.

For the next few days, Noma and I drove through Ipskunk, which was about a two-hundred-house town, and Grand Skid, which was a small city, and Uppington, and Skaggton, and about a dozen other towns. Every time we passed a likely store, I would jump out and investigate. Noma preferred to sit in the car resting her knees. We found out, of course, that any regular store that sold clocks didn't have any glow-in-the-dark models with radium. All they had were plug-in digital clocks. Only antique stores and auction houses had the clocks that we wanted. Sometimes I would find eleven or twelve in one store, and sometimes just one. Luckily they weren't expensive. At the end of each day we'd come home with the back seat of the car clattering with old clocks. Then in the evening we would pry open the front of each clock and scrape the glowing green stuff into a cup, and Dad would pour the cup into the fuel tank, which was a steel gas tank from a tractor. After about three days Dad said that we had enough. He stuck a twig into the fuel tank to see how full it was, and when he was satisfied he screwed the cover back on. He said that a little bit of nuclear fuel would get us a long way, and since we were only going to the moon and hopefully back again, we didn't need a full tank. We were ready to launch.

It was the last day of December, and Noma suggested that we wait until midnight. Our launch would be our New Year's celebration. We would be like a firecracker shooting up into the air. I hoped we wouldn't explode.

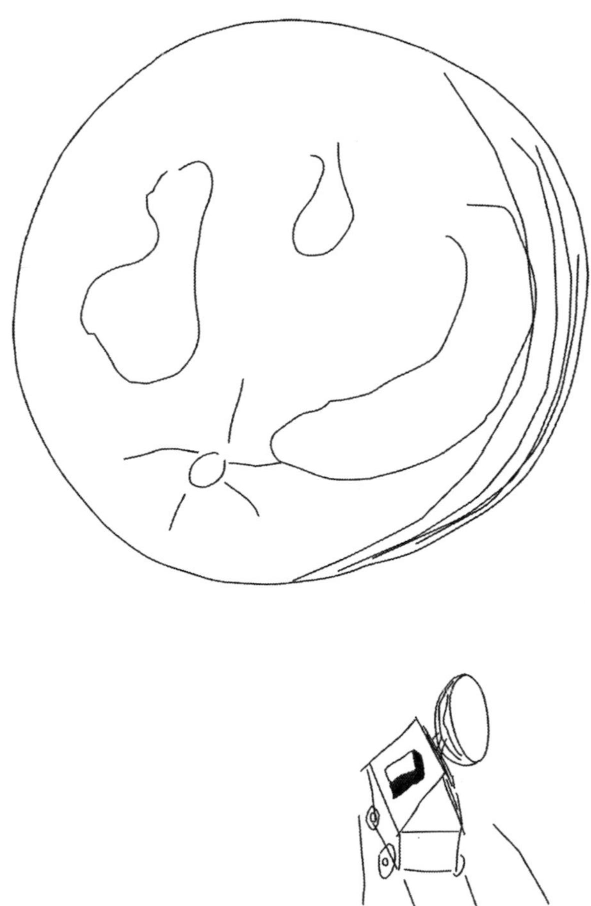

Toward the moon.

14

We climbed through the hatch into the interior. It was surprisingly comfortable. Dad had put an old car seat in the wagon, and up front, for the driver, a reclining chair with a footrest. It was a big wagon, so we had a lot of room, even with Dad in there with us. We had a Styrofoam ice chest packed with cold chicken and egg salad. Under the seat we had a few sacks of potatoes for Dad, and we had some gallon jugs of water for all of us. We had a lot of other stuff in a trunk strapped on the roof, such as Dad's two boxes of papers and a stack of books and some extra clothes, but we couldn't get to the trunk without going outside the ship, which didn't seem likely in space. Maybe it would be possible once we reached the moon. According to Dad, space was very cold, but he had insulated the spaceship with the arctic survival quilt, and so we should be okay. Leonardo had suggested goose feathers, but probably our way was better.

We sat down and buckled ourselves in. Dad closed the hatch, and all the nighttime sounds of creaking trees and hooting night birds stopped suddenly. We were sealed in. I looked out the window at Noma's tiny slate-roofed house in the moonlight. Snow was falling softly through the still air, piling up on the roof and the front steps. The night looked peaceful.

Dad sat in the driver's seat surrounded by about thirty levers and handles and knobs. I hoped he knew which was which. "Here goes," he said, and yanked down on a leather strap. I gritted my teeth and waited for the blast to shoot us up in the air, but nothing happened.

"Um, Dad," I said, "are you sure there's enough fuel?"

"Of course there is," he said. "It's working beautifully."

I looked out the window and realized that we had already left the ground. Leonardo's design didn't involve rocket engines blasting us off the Earth. It was more sophisticated. We rose up gently above Noma's house, through the falling snow, and soon reached the cloud cover. It looked like a giant gray amoeba looming over us, glowing from the moon behind it. We plunged into it and when we came out on top, we were in the clearest, brightest, starriest night I had ever seen.

"There's the moon," Dad said, pointing out the front window. "Somebody hold the map and make sure I'm driving the right way." He handed back a drawing of the moon with an X at our destination. All the moon's craters and pocks and streaks were neatly drawn on the map.

Dad took hold of the controls with his hands and feet and drove straight at the moon. It was a beautiful smooth ride, not like a bumpy car ride over a country road, and certainly nothing like the jerking, stop-and-go movement of a New York taxi. The Earth sped away behind us and the moon loomed bigger and bigger.

"I do wish I had brought a pack of cards," Noma said.

We said nothing for a long time after that. We were too busy looking out the window at the stars.

We had left at midnight, past my usual bedtime, and I fell asleep about an hour later. When I woke up we were still driving. The moon looked bigger. Dad said I had slept for about five hours and it was morning now. We ate breakfast, and then Noma took out a mystery novel, settled in one corner of the seat with her feet up on the ice chest, and read by the light of the moon. I wished I had thought to bring a book. I had nothing to do but look out the window, and although a spread of stars is an amazing thing, it was pretty much all the same. A long trip does get dull.

"Are we there yet, Dad?" I said.

"Oh stop it," he said. "Not for a while."

"What's the moon like? Is it hot? Should I have brought my shorts?"

"I suppose it's hot in the sun and cold in the shade. But it's nothing like you ever learned about in school. I can tell you that."

"I never learned anything about it in school," I said.

"That's not a surprise," he said. "I don't know what they teach you there. How to stick your brain in a blender. If it was up to me. . . ."

I sensed another lecture on imagination coming at me, and I tried to head it off. "Tell me about the moon, Dad."

"The moon?" he said. "There's things the government doesn't want anyone to know. I saw some of the moon files when I was working for Spork. About forty years ago, when NASA was trying to land people on the moon, the first thing they did was to send an unmanned lander. Not too many people know about that lander. It came down picture perfect, and sat on its eight feet, and started filming. But it didn't last more than two minutes. A tentacle whipped out from behind a rock, smacked into the camera lens, and Bam! Crack! Static. Nothing more. That was it. They never got any more photos from that lander. They never found it again."

"Come on, Dad," I said. "There wasn't any tentacle on the moon."

"How do *you* know?" he said. "You never believe me, and then I turn out to be right. I'm telling you Jem, it was a tentacle."

"What color was it?"

"You're testing me," Dad said. "The photos were black and white, so I don't know what color it was. But we'd better be careful up there. We'd better be ready to take off quick, if we see anything we don't understand. And we better not get too near any big rocks if we don't know what's hiding behind them."

"Dad," I said, "every animal I know of that has a tentacle lives in the ocean. So how many oceans are on the moon?"

"Clever," Dad said. "But data trumps cleverness. I saw the film, and I saw the tentacle. I hope we don't get smacked by that thing, but if we do, you'll see it for yourself."

After lunch, Noma and I played hangman and tic-tac-toe on the back of the moon map. She beat me almost every time. She wanted to draw out a chessboard and use little scraps of paper for the pieces, but I got the idea that she would beat me at that too, so I said I was tired, and took a nap. When I woke up, it was time for dinner and we handed out the cold chicken and raw potatoes.

After dinner, Dad tied down the controls, which he said was Leonardo's version of cruise control, and stretched out on the reclining chair. "Everybody get a good sleep," he said. "We should get there tomorrow morning."

When I opened my eyes, I panicked. We must have slept a long time without any regular daylight to wake us. Nobody had thought to set an alarm clock, and now the moon was gigantic, looming in front of us. "Dad!" I shouted. "Wake up! We're gonna crash!"

"Huh?" he said, sitting up suddenly. "I won't! You can't make me, Spork! I quit!"

"Dad, hurry up," I shouted. "Look at the moon!"

Then he woke up all the way. "Oh right," he said, chuckling. "Don't worry. We have a few hours yet. But thanks. We'd better start paying attention if we want to land at the right spot."

For the next three hours we all three stared at the map and stared at the moon, and pointed this way and that, and argued over exactly the right direction, and Dad slowed down the ship considerably so that we could have time to maneuver. Leonardo had specified a flat spot in the middle of a gigantic crater. We lowered our spaceship down into the crater, and all we could see was the blinding white sand of the walls rising up around us. Leonardo had suggested holding up a sheet of smoked glass at this stage of the journey, but Dad handed around sunglasses instead. We set down and I could hear the sand and gravel crunching under the wheels of the wagon.

"Now," Dad said, "let's drive around. Keep your eyes peeled for any sign of Leon."

15

The open plain was so bright that I had trouble seeing clearly even with my sunglasses. After we had driven around for a while, I thought I spotted something nearby in the sand. "Are those rocks, Dad, or what? They look kind of regularly spaced."

Dad drove up closer and we could see that it wasn't rocks. It was a row of indentations in the sand. They looked like footprints.

"Are they tentacle prints?" Dad said anxiously. "Noma, can you recognize animal tracks?"

Noma stared at the prints, squinting out of her old eyes, and then shook her head and said, "How strange. They look just like bear prints. The foot is elongated and ends in a set of claws."

"Wow!" Dad said. "I'd be surprised to find a bear walking around on the moon. But I've been surprised before. Bears are migratory, but I don't see how one could migrate right off the Earth. What if it's a man, and he forgot to clip his toenails? Let's say Leonardo lived up here for two or three years, and forgot to bring a nail clipper with him."

"Dad," I said, "that's ridiculous. He would have invented a nail clipper out of a rock."

"Not necessarily," Dad said. "Maybe he was too busy. I think we're looking at the last footprints of Leonardo, preserved for five hundred years because there's no weather up here to wipe them out."

"But," I said, "how did he walk across the sand without dying from the lack of atmosphere?"

"He could have been holding his breath," Dad said. "He got so bored sitting in his spaceship, looking at the moonscape through a window, year after year, that he finally climbed out to walk around. He held his breath as long as he could, and we'll find his mummified body at the end of the trail."

"But the trail's about a mile long!" I said. "Look at it! It goes right out of sight! How could he hold his breath for so long? Especially with toenails like that, he wouldn't be able to walk very quickly."

"I suggest," Noma said gently, interrupting our argument, "that we follow the trail and find out."

So we did. Dad drove slowly alongside the prints and we tracked them across the open plain. After a while we saw a dark blob far up ahead.

"What's that?" I said.

"Let's be careful," Dad said. "It might only be his mummy. But if I see any tentacles, I'm driving straight up and getting us out of here."

The closer we got, the less like tentacles it looked. But it also didn't look like a mummy. It was standing upright and looked hairy all over.

"Do you think," Dad said in a hushed voice, "it's an orangutan?"

"I think it's a bear," Noma said.

"No!" I said, suddenly understanding. "Dad! Noma! Look! It's a man in a bear suit! It's a spacesuit made out of a bearskin!"

"By God, Jem, you're right!" Dad shouted.

We were close enough that we could see the person clearly, standing and waving at us. He seemed to beckon us to follow him. Then he turned and continued walking across the white sand.

Dad drove slowly behind him.

"Is this a good idea, Dad?" I said in a low voice. "We don't know who's been flying to the moon lately. That could be anybody."

"Don't worry, Jem," Dad said. "I bet he's from the Russian space program. I hear they've run out of money for regular space suits. He might be able to give us information."

In a few minutes we reached a hill that had an

open cave in its side. As soon as we had followed him into the cave, the man pulled a lever on the cave wall and a door slid down behind us, blocking the entrance. The cave had glass-covered windows that let in the light, so we could still see okay. In fact, we could see much better, because the light wasn't too bright for our eyes anymore. The man in the bear suit pulled a second lever, and we heard a giant rushing sound like a tornado. The wagon shook around us in a blast of wind, and then everything was still and silent again.

The man reached up and took off the bear head. When his own head came out from underneath, he was so hairy that he still looked like a bear. His head and chin and cheeks and eyebrows were covered in gray shag that shook loose from the helmet and tumbled down to his elbows. I could see his eyes gleaming far back in the tangle of hair. He seemed to be able to breathe okay.

Dad opened the airlock of our spaceship and we climbed out. Dad stepped over to the man and held out his gigantic long arm. "Greetings, Cosmonaut!" he said. "I'm Carl! Carl Martin. Who are you?"

"Leonardo," the man said, reaching out to shake hands. "Leonardo da Vinci. How do you do?"

16

We were silent for a moment, frozen in astonishment, while the hairy man looked at each of us curiously. Dad began to stammer, "But. . . . Five hundred years. . . . Did you invent a. . . ."

"Please," Leonardo said, "let's step into the living room. It's more comfortable."

He walked to a door in the side of the cave and opened it for us. We still didn't move. I was so surprised I couldn't say a word. Finally Dad staggered toward the door, gripping his head between his hands, and I followed Dad. Noma was the only one of us who remained calm. She smiled politely at Leonardo.

We stepped into a neatly furnished living room. The couch and chairs were made out of carved rocks and didn't look very comfortable. They had fabrics draped over them for style. A low coffee table in the middle of the room held a plateful of cookies. I hoped the cookies weren't carved out of rocks too, because I was hungry. On the far side of the room, a large screen TV was set against the wall. At first I thought the room was covered in wallpaper, but then I realized that it was painted. I could see at a glance that, whoever the current occupant of the room may be, Leonardo da Vinci must have actually painted those murals. Nobody else could have captured the moonscape so realistically, with the Earth hanging round and blue in the sky.

"Have a seat," he said.

We sat down, Dad filling up the entire couch. The man sat in a chair opposite to Dad. It made a strange combination, a giant orangutan on one side of the room and a hairy old man in a bear suit on the other side.

"Look here!" Dad burst out angrily. "Who are you really? You're an imposter! Da Vinci lived five hundred years ago! How can you be him?"

The man nodded his head politely. I could see him smiling behind his beard. "True," he said. "Very puzzling. I might say, similarly, that Sumatran orangutans do not talk. How, then, can you exist?"

Dad stared with his mouth open.

"Ah," the man said gently, holding up his hand. "As I have heard the French say, touché. I would love to hear how you arrived at such an interesting state, and then of course to sketch you. As to my own longevity, it is easily explained. On Earth, it transpires, the gravitational force pulls on the body and ages it rapidly. In the lesser gravity of the moon, the human body degenerates more slowly. By my calculations, I have aged approximately five years since I arrived on the lunar surface."

"But," I said, piping up. "Mr. da Vinci, I didn't know you could speak English?"

"A fair point," he said. "I learned it on TV."

"Ah ha!" my dad shouted, thrusting out his hairy hand and pointing. "You *are* an imposter! If you're really Leo, then how'd you get hold of that TV?"

The man chuckled. "Oh, I built it, of course. About forty years ago, a spacecraft landed not too far from here. It seemed to be uninhabited. I confess, I snuck up on it and knocked it out of commission by hitting it with a whip. I did not know if it was hostile or friendly and I worried that it might harm me. When I was certain that it no longer functioned, I carried it home and built a television out of the parts. Once I was able to receive transmissions from the Earth, I learned a great deal about your current affairs, and also became proficient in several languages. It is a fascinating tool for the transmission of knowledge. Listen to this." He tilted back his head and bellowed, "IT'S THE FLINTSTONES! MEET THE FLINTSTONES! WITH A YABBA DABBA DO ALL DAY!!!"

I clamped my hands over my ears at that horrible noise, and Dad leaped up out of his seat and shouted, "All right! We get the point!"

"Leonardo," Noma said, "people call me Nomasis. Do you know what that means?"

Leonardo stared at her in wonder. "My little grandmother," he said. "I have not heard that language in a long time. Yes, I lived among the Mahicans. They were wonderful people. Did you find my cave and my notebook?"

After that, I was convinced that the man really was Leonardo da Vinci and not an imposter. Dad, however, needed one more proof. He ran out to our wagon, dug through the trunk strapped on the roof, and came back with the framed sketch of da Vinci.

The man looked at the picture in astonishment. "I know that sketch," he said. "I drew it myself." And although he was hairier now, and his face was more creased, he was recognizably the same person as in the portrait.

Our quest was over. We had found the final resting place of Leonardo.

At first we meant to stay a few weeks and then go back home. Dad and Leonardo had a lot to talk about, since they were both inventors, and they wanted to swap ideas before we left. But as time went on, we realized that we liked living on the moon.

Noma was very old. Back on Earth, she had less than ten years to live. But on the moon, by Leonardo's calculations, she might last another thousand years. And besides, she loved the moon. She would take the wagon out and drive around at top speed, zipping all over the lunar surface like a crazy person, practicing wheelies, jumping off of natural rock ramps, and exploring new craters. Sometimes she packed supplies and went out for two or three days at a time.

Dad wasn't very keen on going back to Earth either, because he would have to face more discrimination against talking orangutans. He would never be able to find a respectable job or go out in public without attracting unwanted attention.

As for me, if I went back, I would have to go to school. I liked school, and I generally liked learning new things. But in the secret lunar laboratory of Leonardo da Vinci, I could learn an incredible amount. By his estimates, I had about eight thousand more years to improve my mind.

I was worried that Leonardo might have gotten used to living alone and might not want so much company. But he didn't seem to mind. He and Dad spent all day in the laboratory room talking and arguing and inventing new things. The last I heard, they were going to dig out the center of the moon and start a giant bat colony.

I have about eight thousand years ahead of me in low gravity. That's a lot of time to explore. Maybe someday I'll fly the spaceship off the moon and visit the rest of the galaxy, in search of aliens. As Dad says, once you free up your imagination, there's no knowing how far you can go. We're living proof of it.

The Author

B. B. Wurge began writing children's books after leaving his first career as an entertainer in a primate house. He says, "I've been told the world is crazy, more now than ever. That may be true, but children should know they can navigate successfully through our crazy world if they stick to fundamental principles: loyalty to family and friends, compassion, and an open imagination." Wurge holds degrees in hair growth and zoology. He lives in an elevator in Manhattan.

About the Type

This book was set in Adobe Caslon, a typeface originally released by William Caslon in 1722. His types became popular throughout Europe and the American colonies, and printer Benjamin Franklin used hardly any other typeface. The first printings of the American Declaration of Independence and the Constitution were set in Caslon. For her Caslon revival for Adobe, designer Carol Twombly studied specimen pages printed by William Caslon between 1734 and 1770.

Designed by John Taylor-Convery
Composed at JTC Imagineering, Santa Maria, CA